THEIR TRAIL LED TO CASPER

Smith—his music brought beauty to the concert halls of Europe. Now he's a man on the run—from a violent past.

Amy Coaltree—drawn to the beauty of the West, repelled by its brutality. Will she have to choose between a father she's never met and a man she's determined to love?

West DuMont—many people call his boss, Ben Coaltree, ruthless. But DuMont's getting ready to show them what ruthlessness really means.

Fast Charlie Payson—he kills for money, for whiskey, for fun. Sometimes he kills just to show he's the fastest there is.

Angus Hightower—he's playing a dangerous, high-stakes game. His life, and the life of the town, will depend on who wins.

The Stagecoach Series
Ask your bookseller for the books you have missed

STAGECOACH STATION 36:
CASPER

Hank Mitchum

Created by the producers of
Wagons West, White Indian,
Badge, and Winning the West.

Book Creations Inc., Canaan, NY · Lyle Kenyon Engel, Founder

BANTAM BOOKS
TORONTO · NEW YORK · LONDON · SYDNEY · AUCKLAND

STAGECOACH STATION 36: CASPER

*A Bantam Book / published by arrangement with
Book Creations, Inc.*

Bantam edition / July 1988

*Produced by Book Creations, Inc.
Lyle Kenyon Engel: Founder*

ISBN 0-553-27271-3

Published simultaneously in the United States and Canada

*Bantam Books are published by Bantam Books, a division of
Bantam Doubleday Dell Publishing Group, Inc. Its trademark,
consisting of the words "Bantam Books" and the portrayal of
a rooster, is Registered in U.S. Patent and Trademark Office
and in other countries. Marca Registrada. Bantam Books,
666 Fifth Avenue, New York, New York 10103.*

STAGECOACH STATION 36:

CASPER

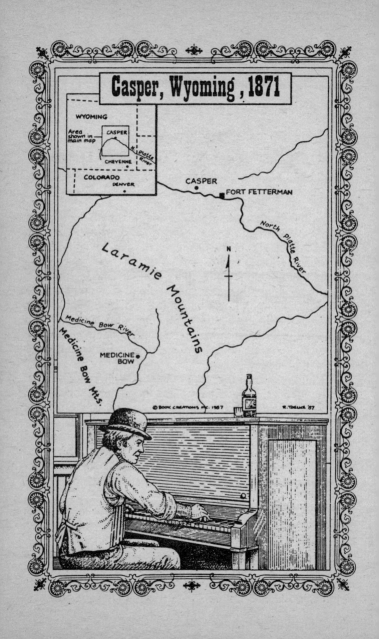

Prologue:
A Kansas Cow Town in 1869

The sound of a silver coin being slapped on the bar made the saloonkeeper look around. The young man who had just put the coin down was waiting to be served. He was wearing a black hat with a silver headband, from which a small red feather protruded. Hanging low in a quick-draw holster on the right side of a bullet-studded belt was a Colt .44, silver plated, its grip inlaid with mother-of-pearl. The man was slender, with dark hair and dark eyes, and there was a gracefulness about the way he walked and moved. He carried himself with an effortless economy of motion.

Without being asked, the bartender served the best whiskey the saloon had to offer. A few moments earlier, as the young man had ridden on horseback down Center Street, news had spread quickly that the famous gunfighter Rufus Butler was in town, and the bartender did not want to offend him by serving bad liquor. Rufus was said to be as quick as thought and deadlier than a rattlesnake; many a would-be shootist had gone down before his gun.

Rufus thanked the bartender with a slight nod and then slowly surveyed the interior of the saloon. It was typical of the many he had seen over the past five years. Wide, rough-hewn boards formed the plank floor, and against the wall behind the long, brown-stained bar was a shelf of whiskey bottles, their number doubled by the mirror they stood against. Half a dozen tables, occupied by a dozen or more men, filled the room, and tobacco smoke hovered under the ceiling like a cloud. It was now twilight, and as daylight disappeared, flickering kerosene lanterns combined with the smoke to make the room seem even hazier.

During the past five years, these kinds of surroundings had somehow become the young man's heritage. He had been redefined by the saloons, cow towns, stables, dusty streets, and open prairies he had encountered. He could not deny them without denying his own existence, and yet, with all that was in him, he wished it were not so.

At the opposite end of the bar stood a tall, bearded man. Watching himself in the mirror, he tossed his drink down and wiped the back of his hand across his mouth. Then he turned to look at Rufus.

"Hey, you."

Rufus did not turn.

"I'm talkin' to you, mister, the fella with the red feather in your hat."

Rufus looked at him and saluted him silently with his drink. He knew from the tone of the voice, though, that the bearded man was not offering him a simple greeting.

"Ain't you Rufus Butler?"

Rufus did not answer.

"You got the silver hatband and red feather, and you got the pearl-handled, silver-plated pistol. You tryin' to make out like you're somebody you ain't?"

"My name is Rufus S. Butler," Rufus said quietly.

"Then you're the one I'm lookin' for . . . *gunfighter*." The bearded man said the word with a sneer.

Rufus looked away from him and stared into the mirror above the rows of bottles. The other people in the saloon, recognizing the escalating challenge, began to move out of the way. Like a macabre ballet, the intricate dance of death had already begun.

Rufus closed his eyes for a moment and, by force of will, transported himself away. In his mind's eye he saw himself elegantly dressed, seated at a piano on the stage of a large theater in London, Paris, or Vienna. But he could not hear the music. *Where was the music?*

"Tell me, Rufus, is it true you killed more men than you can count?" the bearded man taunted, his grating voice louder and more threatening now.

Rufus opened his eyes. The theater, the piano, and Paris vanished. He was here, in a foul-smelling saloon in a Kansas town whose name he had not yet bothered to learn. He looked in the mirror again and saw that everyone had moved out of the line of fire except two men. They were sitting at tables on opposite sides of the room from each other, drinking whiskey and making a point of not looking at Rufus or the bearded man. Probably making an effort not to spook either one of the principals, was the impression Rufus had.

He put the whiskey glass down with a tired sigh and turned to face his tormentor.

"Mister, you don't really want to do this, do you?" he asked. It was more than a question; it was almost a plea.

The bearded man stepped away from the bar and flipped his coat back so that the handle of his pistol was exposed. "Yeah," the man answered defiantly. "Yeah, I do wanna do it."

Rufus studied the man's eyes. Having been center stage in variations of this deadly dance too many times now, he knew that the eyes never lied. They told him how frightened or confident his adversary was, where he was going to shoot, and, what was more important, when he was going to make his move.

When Rufus first looked into the bearded man's eyes, he was somewhat confused. The eyes gleamed with a wild, unaccountable confidence. Where did that confidence come from? It was not a confidence of skill. It was . . . suddenly Rufus knew! Though the bearded man was performing the opening steps, it was not solely his creation, this dance. Someone else had helped choreograph his moves.

Rufus glanced in the mirror and saw that the two men at the tables had already pulled their pistols from their holsters. They were hiding them, holding them down in their laps, ready for the fight to begin.

Rufus let out a slow breath. Now that he knew what was

in store for him, he relaxed. He waited easily for the bearded man to move into the violent scene that Rufus knew from experience would come next.

"Let's go!" the bearded man suddenly shouted, reaching awkwardly for his gun.

But Rufus's greatest danger was from the two men at the tables; as he turned toward them, their guns were already blazing. Bullets crashed into the bar beside him, and glass exploded on the shelves behind. Rufus brought his gun up and fired twice, dispatching his two bullets with deadly accuracy toward the two men, who had attempted to make the feat more difficult by positioning themselves on opposite sides of the room.

The first gunman took a bullet between his eyes and was pitched backward, dead before he hit the floor. The second gunman was hit in the chest and thrown from his chair. He slammed against the wall and then slid down, painting a swath of blood on the wainscoting behind him.

Rufus swung back to the bearded man, who, stunned by Rufus's speed, was just now clearing leather. Rufus sent a .44 caliber ball crashing into the man's heart, killing him instantly.

A thick layer of gun smoke swirled through the room, mixing with the tobacco haze to form an obscuring cloud. Rufus knew that if others were after him, they would have the advantage of being partially hidden by the smoke. He had to get out. Holding his pistol out in front of him, he backed slowly across the room, feeling behind him with his hand until he reached the batwing doors. He pushed the swinging panels open and backed out onto the wooden porch.

Rufus heard the deadly, metallic click of a gun being cocked directly behind him. Expecting a fourth gunman, he whirled and fired in one fluid motion, and then he looked in shock and horror at a small boy grabbing his chest, trying to hold back the blood that was squirting through his fingers. The boy fell backward off the porch and lay sprawled in the street in front of the saloon, his eyes open but already glazed with death. The boy's gun, an old broken Remington used as a plaything, lay in the dirt beside him.

"My God, mister, you just killed a little kid," someone on Center Street called to him.

Half a dozen people came running from the saloon, while an equal number moved toward him from the town's main street. Rufus looked at their shocked, accusing faces.

"I . . . I'm sorry," he said. "I didn't know. He came up behind me and cocked his gun. I thought it was . . ." His voice trailed off.

Numbly, he slipped his gun into its holster and then mounted his horse and pointed it out of town. Heedless of his safety now, he waited for a bullet in the back, almost praying that one would come. But no one in the crowd lifted a finger to stop him.

Slowly, Rufus Butler rode off alone into the gathering darkness, never once looking back.

Chapter One

It was two o'clock in the morning when Ben Coaltree dumped the packet of letters on his desk and then adjusted the kerosene lantern to the desired brightness. For the past six months he had been reading his mail at this hour because it allowed him the opportunity to be alone, with no chance of being disturbed. A private mail pouch was sent to him each week from San Francisco via his own stage line.

Contained in this week's pouch was a letter of agreement, finalizing his purchase of the Central Coach Line. Ben had bought the assets of Central for just under one hundred thousand dollars. In a last-ditch effort to prevent the sale, two directors of the bankrupt company had sued in U.S. circuit court in Denver to declare the transaction illegal. But they had lost their fight, and now seventy-five coaches and twelve hundred miles of new stage routes had come under Ben Coaltree's control.

There was also a bill of sale from the Abbot-Downing Company for thirty new coaches, shipped on flatcars on a single train to Salt Lake City. These coaches were to be used in service over the Sierra Nevadas, by way of Placerville and Virginia City. The coaches were like beautiful gems, and the shipment, including spare parts and sixty harnesses, was valued at forty-five thousand dollars.

There were half a dozen letters from newspapers, requesting that he grant them interviews. Every mail pouch contained at least that number, and as usual Ben discarded them without giving them serious consideration.

A United States congressman had written to say that every one of his votes on the transportation bills that had come before the House this session had favored the Coaltree Cross-country Express Company. Ben read through the letter:

"As you well know, Mr. Coaltree, this entire country is enamored of the railroad and would have Congress pass laws so favorable to the rail industry that coach and wagon lines would soon go out of business. I, however, have always looked out for your interest. Therefore it does not seem unreasonable to me that I should ask for a rather sizable contribution to my next campaign."

After tossing that letter into the pile with the newspaper interview requests, Ben began to go through the rest of the letters, most of which seemed to be from the general public. His company got hundreds of such letters every month, and he had requested to see a representative sampling of them. Most were complaints about service, which Ben generally regarded as the normal complaints everyone had about institutions that were bigger than life. Occasionally, however, there would be a letter complimenting one of his drivers, or thanking him personally for providing service to an area that would otherwise have been isolated.

One of the envelopes had a note attached to it, and this caught his attention. The note was from Percy Rawlings, his business manager: "Mr. Coaltree, please notice the name and return address on this letter. It may be only a coincidence, but I thought you should see it."

Ben looked at the envelope and then gasped. The return address was Amy Coaltree, Chestnut Street, Boston, Massachusetts.

Could it be true? After twenty-two years, had he finally

heard from his daughter? His fingers trembling in excitement, he opened the letter.

March 15, 1871

Dear Father,

I have no right to call you that, except by right of birth. I have not really been a daughter to you, as I have never made an effort to contact you before now.

My only excuse is that I thought it would be painful to my mother if she thought I tried to write to you. I have long wondered what you were like, however, and I have always harbored a desire to see your magnificent West.

It is with regret that I tell you that Mother passed away two weeks ago. She enjoyed good health for all of her life, but contracted a chill last winter and expired before spring's thaw could exert its healing influence upon her. I shall miss her greatly, but am comforted by the promise of our Lord to keep in His loving arms all who have professed their faith in Him.

I would like to visit you. If this is possible, please answer this letter and tell me where and how to find you.

Sincerely,
Amy.

Ben reached up, extinguished the lantern, and then sat in the dark for several long minutes. He was particularly glad to be alone at this moment. He did not want anyone to see him cry.

The immigrant car on the *Omaha Flyer* was little more than a converted freight car, with hard springs that let it toss and jerk on the track bed like a small vessel at sea. Despite its swaying motion, the conductor walked through it with confident strides. A little girl pulled at his trousers, but the child's mother snatched her back. A bearded old man with a long-stemmed pipe shifted his legs to clear the aisle.

Ranked below second-class accommodations, the immigrant car on this westbound Union Pacific train was crowded with over forty persons; strangely dressed men, stoic women, and noisy, active children en route to new lands and new homes late in the spring of 1871. Denied access to the dining car, these passengers prepared their own meals, and as they were now sitting down to supper, the car reeked with the mingled aromas of cold sausage, garlic, and sauerkraut. The food odors, combined with the smoke of cheap pipe tobacco and the sour smell of bodies that had gone unwashed for several days, made the immigrant car a very unpleasant place to be.

The conductor hurried through the car and then proceeded at a more moderate pace through the second-class and first-class cars, and finally he passed through the dining car and arrived in the Wagner Palace Car. Just as the immigrant car was below second class, the Wagner Palace Car was above first class. Here no expense was spared to make the passengers' journey pleasant. The chairs were deeply cushioned, the carpets were plush, and the woodwork was varnished. At the windows were velvet curtains, and the ornate light fixtures hanging from the ceiling glistened.

There were only five people in the Palace Car, two married couples and a beautiful young woman who was traveling alone. The lone woman, in her early twenties, had a fair, fine complexion, and the ghost of a recent exposure to the sun could be seen in her few remaining freckles. The conductor had been told who she was when she changed trains in Omaha. Her name was Amy Coaltree, and, he had been instructed, she was to be treated with special consideration—an order he resented, because he treated *everyone* on the Palace Car with special consideration.

He cleared his throat discreetly to announce his ap-

proach. "Is there anything I can get for you, Miss Coaltree?"
he asked.

Amy smiled prettily at him. "No, thank you, I'm just
fine," she said.

"Your dinner will be ready shortly."

"Thank you."

When the conductor moved on to the others in the car,
Amy turned back to face the window. They were three-
quarters of the way across Nebraska, and there was nothing to see outside but miles of open prairie. Amy was
crossing this vast emptiness to get to Casper, Wyoming,
where she would meet her father, whom she had never
seen. Amy, raised in the genteel and privileged chambers
of Boston society, was facing a new life, now that her
mother had died. But rather than anticipating the prospect with anxiety, she was looking forward to it, and her
eagerness to embrace this change was reflected in the
diary she had recently begun to keep. She picked up the
green, leather-bound daybook and resumed writing:

There is no other way to describe what I am
seeing outside my window than to say we are at sea.
That may sound strange, as there is no sea in Nebraska, but I'm not speaking of a sea of water and
rolling waves. Rather, this is a sea of grass, sky, and
earth, totally devoid of the hand of man, save the
twin steel rails that stretch front and back from horizon to horizon, glistening in the sun. From side to
side there is but the green plain, vast and empty,
touched by the blue skirts of heaven.

Mrs. Adams and Mrs. Poindexter, who are also on
this car, have complained bitterly of the drab scenery. I think it is only because they aren't looking.
I've seen wildflowers of many hues and designs growing in colorful profusion on both sides of the track. I
also often see in the distance tiny dots, which grow
more and more distinct as we draw near, until they
reveal themselves to be strange little houses, constructed entirely of mud and sod. Then, too quickly,

we flash by them, and they recede behind us, until they are indistinguishable from the ground from which they sprung.

A uniformed steward approached Amy's chair and said, "Excuse me, Miss Coaltree, but your table is ready."

"Thank you," Amy responded. She was hungry, and the meals so far had been excellent, but she always approached the trip to the dining car with trepidation. She drew a deep breath, as if about to plunge into an icy stream, and opened the rear door of the parlor car. As soon as she stepped out onto the platform she felt as if she had entered another world. The noise was tremendous, and the wind whipped against her dress and hair. The car's normal rocking motion was greatly exaggerated here, and she held onto the railing to keep from being thrown off.

Between the platforms of the two cars was a gap, narrow enough to be stepped across but wide enough so that with just a misstep an unfortunate passenger could drop onto the tracks below. Although she had already negotiated the gap many times during the trip, Amy still approached it with as much caution as she had the first time.

She stood there for a moment, feeling the rhythm of the car and looking down to make certain that the heights of the platforms were equal before she stepped off. Then, timing her move, she stepped across and opened the door to the dining car. As soon as she stepped inside, she was met by a waiter.

"Your table is ready," he said. "Right this way, please."

Amy perused a menu that featured blue-winged teal, antelope steaks, roast beef, boiled ham and tongue, broiled chicken, corn on the cob, fresh fruit, hot rolls, and corn bread. She could feel her appetite gradually returning as she mulled over the choices. Boiled ham might be good, she thought, and she motioned to the waiter.

There was a rush of activity in Medicine Bow when the stagecoach, a beautiful shiny black one, rolled into town unexpectedly at noon. The driver was wearing a bright red coat, and the shotgun guard was possibly the biggest man ever to be seen in town. Since no coach was due at this time, the arrival of such a grand one created a great deal of attention.

Medicine Bow, which existed solely because of the railroad, was not a prepossessing town. It had only two streets, one that ran parallel with the track, another that ran perpendicular to it, forming a T with the first. The Medicine Bow Hotel stood on a corner where the two streets met, and it faced the railroad track. The train depot was on the opposite side of the track.

The coach stopped in front of the hotel, and the driver and shotgun guard climbed down from the box to open the door. The Medicine Bow Hotel boasted a front porch and a dozen rocking chairs, which were usually occupied. Many of the people in them were so interested in this stagecoach that they risked losing their prized rocking chairs to others in order to get a closer look at it. Those already present at the hotel were joined by a dozen or so more, who had seen the coach arrive and now drifted toward it to see who would be riding in such an elegant rig.

A slender, darkly handsome young man stepped out of the coach. He wore a brown suit and a fedora, and he carried a silver-headed cane. He looked around at the little town, his face registering obvious distaste at its lack of amenities.

"Mr. Meeker," the young man said, turning toward the huge shotgun guard.

"Yes, sir, Mr. DuMont?" the giant answered.

"Would you please see to our accommodations for the night? I must send a telegram."

"Yes, sir," Meeker said, and he stepped up onto the porch and went inside the hotel. He was at least six feet, nine inches tall, with huge shoulders, a barrel chest, and arms as big as most men's legs. He was completely bald, and his neck was so heavily muscled that it was impossible to tell where it left off and his shoulders began. Most of the citizens of Medicine Bow had never seen anyone like him, and they followed him inside and looked on with unabashed curiosity.

When the huge man named Meeker was in the hotel, Wes DuMont asked one of the gawking bystanders where he might find the Western Union office. Upon learning its location, he walked briskly in that direction, swinging his cane as he stepped.

The week before, Wes DuMont had received a letter asking for someone in the Denver office of the Coaltree Cross-country Express Company to meet Ben Coaltree's daughter, Amy, in Medicine Bow. From there she was to be escorted to Casper, where she would be met by her father. Others in the Coaltree organization might have resented such a directive, but Wes DuMont saw it as opportunity knocking. DuMont reasoned that if he made a favorable impression on Ben Coaltree's daughter, he would make a favorable impression upon the man himself. And if the impression were favorable enough, who knew where it might lead?

DuMont was a person who knew how to take advantage of an opportunity. It was a trait he had developed long ago in the orphanage where he had been raised. There DuMont saw that the only way to get ahead in life was to take charge of his own destiny. It started out simply enough. The orphanage always had too many children and too little food, but DuMont made sure that he always got his share, and his share was more than anyone else's.

That trait had carried over into his adult life, and now he enjoyed a position of respect and authority in the Coaltree Cross-country Express Company. Though originally hired as a minor clerk in the Denver office, DuMont had learned that there were advantages to be realized by working for a large organization—so large that the people in the office never saw the owner of the company. Taking advantage of Ben Coaltree's distance from the operation, DuMont forged letters from Coaltree that promoted him to open positions of greater responsibility and higher pay. Thus, his coworkers in Denver believed his promotions to be coming from the office in San Francisco, while the people in San Francisco thought they originated in Denver. DuMont had recently given himself the title of executive secretary to Ben Coaltree. It was a position that he had created for himself, one that carried with it a tremendous amount of power. As executive secretary, DuMont could do virtually anything he wanted in Ben Coaltree's name—without Ben Coaltree's knowledge. DuMont hoped to keep Coaltree in the dark about his actions until he was able to present his employer with a new, successful stage route to add to the company's line. Then, DuMont hoped, Coaltree would be forgiving of his employee's presumption of authority.

DuMont stepped into the Western Union office, located at one end of the depot. The depot was empty, since no trains were due for several hours. The little potbellied stove in the center of the depot was cold because it was the middle of June and the weather was pleasant. The stove had been used as recently as two weeks ago, however, and a box of ashes was still underneath. The door to the stove was open, and the room was perfumed with the smell of stale wood smoke.

DuMont stepped up to the Western Union window and slapped his hand on the counter.

"My good man," he called.

A small, middle-aged man with a hooknose, wire-rimmed glasses, and a green visor shuffled over to the window. "You want to send a telegram?" he asked.

"Yes. I want to send a telegram to a passenger on a Union Pacific train. Is that possible?"

"Yes, of course. Which train?"

"The one arriving here tomorrow morning."

"That would be the *Omaha Flyer*," the clerk said. "When do you want the passenger to get it?"

"As soon as possible."

The telegraph operator picked up a train timetable and consulted the schedule.

"The *Omaha Flyer* will be passing through Broadwater 'bout suppertime. We can get the message on board then. It'll cost extra."

"Cost is no object," DuMont said, taking the pad and writing his message. "Just see to it that the telegram is delivered."

On board the *Omaha Flyer* that evening, Amy Coaltree pushed her dessert plate away, feeling a twinge of shame over having enjoyed it so. "It's a good thing this trip isn't going to last a month," she had confided to her diary just the day before. "For if it did, I would surely grow fat from the delicious food."

"Miss Coaltree?"

"Yes?" Amy looked up to see the train conductor.

"I have a telegram for you," he said, holding out a yellow envelope.

"A telegram for me?"

"Yes. We picked it up for you a few moments ago, when we passed through Broadwater."

"Really? I don't recall stopping." Amy took the envelope.

The conductor smiled proudly. "Why, it isn't necessary to stop," he explained. "We have a device there for snatching messages while we're going by at full speed."

"How exciting! Thank you for delivering it to me," Amy said, and opening the envelope, she read the message inside:

MISS AMY COALTREE
UNION PACIFIC
OMAHA FLYER
SENT FROM MEDICINE BOW 6-15-71 4:30
AS PER INSTRUCTIONS OF YOUR FATHER I WILL MEET
YOU IN MEDICINE BOW STOP MY NAME IS WES DUMONT
STOP WE WILL PROCEED BY PRIVATE COACH FROM MEDI-
CINE BOW TO CASPER STOP I AM HAPPY TO BE OF SERVICE
STOP

When Amy went to bed that night, she lay in her berth, listening to the soothing, steady click-click of steel wheels over rail joints and thinking about tomorrow. She would reach Medicine Bow and be met by Wes DuMont, whoever that might be, and with him go to Casper, where for the first time in her life she would meet her father. It was an exciting prospect, but as the time drew closer she felt nervous butterflies in her stomach.

Amy had been raised and schooled in Boston. Her mother, who had divorced Ben Coaltree when Amy was an infant, had seldom talked about her former husband, though she did say that he was a handsome man and a man of good qualities.

Despite never having seen him, Amy had a burning curiosity about Ben Coaltree. She had made every effort to find out about him, short of actually contacting him, which she had felt would be an affront to her mother. By the time Amy was twelve years old, she knew that her father was a very wealthy man, and she often saw his name in periodicals and newspapers, such as *Harper's Weekly* and the *Boston Evening Transcript*.

"Ben Coaltree has realized man's most treasured dream," one article said. "He has carved an empire from the wilderness, fighting Indians and highwaymen, mountains and wild rivers, to provide transportation for thousands of Western pioneers."

The story went on to tell how the Coaltree Cross-country Express controlled over four thousand miles of stagecoach and express lines, connecting virtually every town and settlement in the West not already connected by railroad. The article made her father into a noble figure, a man of heroic proportions, and that was the image she had of him.

But her father was also a man of mystery. It was said that he was rarely seen, even by his closest associates. He owned a huge mansion on Nob Hill in San Francisco, and some suggested that he had become a recluse, a hermit who never left his house, and thus never got to enjoy the fortune he had amassed.

When Amy reached maturity, her mother had revealed some further information. "I must confess that it was I who wronged your father," Amy's mother told her. "But I could not face the rigors of living in his wild West. Mr. Coaltree would not return to Boston, and I could not in good conscience subject you to such an upbringing. Therefore, on the very night of your birth, I filed for a bill of divorcement. I have never lived down the shame of my action, but I have always felt that what I did was best for you. You have enjoyed the advantages of genteel society. You were sent on a tour of Europe and given a fine education. All that has made you into a proper young lady. I do not think that would have been possible had I stayed married to your father and brought you up under such miserable conditions as were afforded by that wretched country."

This confession had served to strengthen Amy's resolve. She had never shared her secret desire with her mother, but she had always had a craving not only to meet her father but to see his West. She did appreciate the advantages of education and society her mother had provided for her, but there was also buried deep within her a thirst for adventure. She wondered to herself if it were the adventurous blood of her father that made her want to do such things. And she had become desperate to leave Boston and see the rest of the country. That was why, after her mother had died, Amy had written to her father.

She had not been sure that he would answer, or that he even acknowledged her existence. To her happy surprise he not only answered but also sent money, tickets, and instructions for visiting him in Casper, Wyoming, where, he explained, he had recently bought a ranch, not to raise cattle but to have a place to go to "relax and get away from the cares of business."

Amy had been traveling for five days now; tomorrow she would leave the train to start the last leg of her journey. By this time the next night she would be in Casper, Wyoming.

When Amy stepped down from the train the next morning, what she saw made her wonder whether the entire town of Medicine Bow had turned out to meet the train. Half a dozen buckboards and wagons were parked at the depot, and dozens of men, women, and children stood on the platform, just watching the excitement.

The engine, painted green with red trim and high-lighted with shiny brass fittings, released rhythmic puffs of steam through the relief valve, as if exhausted from its efforts. A dozen wide-eyed youngsters stood on the ground beside the engine, looking up at the engineer's cab and at the maze of instruments, pipework, valves, and levers, marveling at the wonderful complexities.

Standing on a box across the platform from the train was a tall thin man dressed in black, with a stovepipe hat that made him appear even taller. He was holding out a brown bottle toward the crowd of people who were standing nearby. "Now, let me tell you about this wonderful Con-stitution Life Syrup," the man was saying. "This magnifi-cent elixir is a positive cure for dyspepsia, scrofula, paralysis, bearing-down feelings, or tainted blood," he declared. "For only fifty cents a bottle, you can be restored to perfect health."

"Or have a pretty good drunk," someone in the crowd shouted, and everyone laughed.

A newspaper boy passed through the crowd shouting the day's headlines. "Federal troops move against night riders in Mississippi!"

"Miss Coaltree?" She had been addressed by a well-dressed, good-looking man. "You are Miss Amy Coaltree?"

"Yes," she said. "How did you know?"

The man smiled. "Why, that's easy. I was told you would be the most beautiful young brunette woman on the train. I'm Wes DuMont. Did you get my telegram?"

"Yes," Amy said. "You are going to take me to my father?"

"I am indeed."

"How far is it to this place . . . to Casper?"

"It's about eight hours by stagecoach," DuMont said. "If you'll just come this way, the coach is right over here."

"My luggage—"

"Mr. Meeker is seeing to it," DuMont said.

Amy glanced toward the baggage car and saw a giant of a man reaching down to pick up her steamer trunk with no more effort than he would for a small valise. He lifted it to his shoulder amid gasps of awe from the young boys who had been admiring the engine.

"I've never seen such a strong man," Amy said.

"Mr. Meeker was once a bareknuckle boxing champion," the tall, slender man said. "I find it useful to have someone like him around."

"You mean as a bodyguard?" Amy asked. "He's your bodyguard?"

"Something like that, yes," DuMont said. "Miss Coaltree, you must remember, this is wild country. That's why your father asked me to meet you here and escort you to Casper."

Amy followed DuMont over to the coach, where a man was standing.

"This is Simmons, our driver."

"Pleased to meet you, Mr. Simmons," Amy said, smiling at him.

Simmons opened the door for them, and first Amy and then DuMont climbed inside. The interior of the coach was upholstered a rich red. The upholstery was not only beautiful, Amy noticed, it was also very comfortable. When Meeker put her steamer trunk in the boot, the back of the coach sank a little under its weight, silent evidence of the giant's great strength. She felt the coach shift again as Meeker climbed up to the seat beside the driver, and then DuMont gave the signal to go.

As the coach began to move, Amy studied the man sitting across from her, though without making it obvious that she was doing so. He was a handsome man; she had to admit that. And so far he had displayed nothing but the most impeccable manners. Yet there was something about him that she found disturbing. He was, she thought, like an exquisite stem of crystal, formed of beautiful material but somehow flawed, as if it were imperfectly crafted. She finally decided that the imperfection was in his eyes. The light she saw there was cold and remote.

They rode in silence for a couple of hours, Amy marveling at the breathtaking vistas of this new country, while DuMont looked through the window quietly and thoughtfully. The only sounds were from the roll of the wheels, the gentle rocking of the coach, the clumping of the horses' hooves, and occasionally a whistle from the driver accompanied by the loud crack of his whip.

Chapter Two

Later that morning, in the small town of Freeland, people were going about their business on the main street when a stranger rode in. He pulled up near the way station, dismounted, and tied his horse to the hitchrail. The townspeople watched him with increasing curiosity as he took off his hat and rubbed a handkerchief across his face. His hair and eyebrows were snow-white, his skin as pale as any skin they had ever seen. He glanced toward them with eyes that had a light pinkish tinge but were otherwise as colorless as glass.

The albino was wearing a gun strapped low on his right hip. He looked around behind him once and then, not appearing to take notice of two stable hands outside the way station, walked past them and went inside.

"You know who that is?" one of the stable hands asked after the albino was through the swinging doors and out of hearing.

"I ain't never seen him," the bearded one answered. "But I've heard him described. That's gotta be—"

"Fast Charlie Payson," the first one interrupted, as though he did not want to be cheated out of saying it.

"I was going to say that," the one with the beard retorted. "I know'd who it was first time I seen him. I didn't need you to tell me."

"What you reckon he's doin' here?"

"Don't know. But if he's lookin' for anyone, I sure wouldn't want to be that person."

21

"Me neither."

Inside the station, Payson stepped up to the bar, and the bartender hurried over to see what he wanted. At the opposite end of the bar a cowboy and a young woman were talking and laughing, a bottle of whiskey on the bar in front of them.

"Whiskey," Payson ordered.

"Afraid we got no blended whiskey left," the bartender said. "The cowboy over there bought our last bottle. Got some pretty good trade liquor though."

Payson pointed to the bottle in front of the cowboy. "I'll have his bottle."

"Can't. I told you, the cowboy bought the whole bottle."

"You," Payson said to the cowboy. "I'd be obliged if you'd slide that bottle down this way."

The cowboy smiled and nodded to the bartender, saying, "Pour him a glass on me, Whipple. I just got paid, and I'm feelin' generous."

"I don't want a glass," Payson said. "I want the whole bottle."

"Sorry, mister. I been thinkin' for a month 'bout comin' in here and sharin' a bottle of blended whiskey with my friends. Now if you're callin' yourself my friend, you can have a drink or two, but I'm keepin' the bottle."

Payson walked toward him and started to reach for the bottle. The cowboy put out his hand to stop him.

"Mister, you pick up that bottle and I'm gonna knock you on your ass," the cowboy said menacingly.

Payson grunted with contempt, moved around the cowboy's outstretched hand, and grabbed the neck of the bottle. Before his fingers could wrap securely around it, the cowboy hit him. Payson caught the punch on his jaw and went down to the floor.

The cowboy laughed. "I told you what I was gonna do," he said apologetically, and then reached down to help Payson up. "Now, why don't you just have a drink and forget it?"

Payson stood up and glared at the cowboy. "Pull your gun, mister."

"What?"

"Pull your gun or give me the bottle."

The cowboy looked bewildered. "You want to pull a gun over a bottle of whiskey?"

"Give the bottle to him, Lee," the woman with him said in a frightened voice.

"Hell, no, I ain't gonna give it to him. Mister, I don't know who you are, but if you're wantin' to continue this fight, I reckon I can oblige you."

"Lee, my God, don't you know who this is?" the woman asked, her voice rising with panic. "This is Fast Charlie Payson."

"Don't reckon I've ever heard the name," Lee said, still staring at the albino.

"Lee, this fella may be the fastest man with a gun there ever was," Whipple spoke up from behind the bar.

"I'm a workin' cowboy, Whipple," Lee said. "I don't get around enough to hear about who's supposed to be good with a gun. But I don't reckon it matters none, 'cause I ain't plannin' on fightin' him." Lee reached for the bottle. "I'll be takin' my bottle with me. I'll come back when the company's a little better."

"You won't reach your horse alive," Payson warned.

"You gonna shoot me in the back?"

"Could be."

Bottle in hand, Lee started for the door while Payson watched him. The two stable hands peering over the batwing doors from outside moved to let Lee come through. The albino followed him.

"You ain't goin' nowhere, mister," Payson said.

On the porch Lee turned to face him. "I'm riding out of here," he said.

"I'll make it easy on you," Payson said. "I'm going to count to three. You can pull your gun anytime you want, but you better do it before I get to three 'cause that's when I'm pulling mine."

"I . . . I don't want to do this," Lee said in a frightened voice.

"You ain't got no choice," Payson said. "One . . ."

Lee gave a resigned sigh and set the bottle down.

"Two."

Lee made a desperate grab for his pistol. Payson smiled at him and waited for Lee to clear leather before he even started for his own gun. Then, as Lee was still bringing his pistol up, Payson drew. His shoulder jumped, and the gun appeared in his hand, already blazing. The bullet caught Lee in the chest and pitched him back off the porch and into the dirt. His arms flopped uselessly beside him, the trigger finger on his gunhand still jerking in response to his last conscious thought, even though he had dropped the gun and his hand was empty.

The two stable hands walked over to look down at Lee's body. Lee's feet, covered by well-worn boots, were turned out at an unusual angle. Whipple joined them. "We can't leave him here," Whipple growled.

"What do you want to do with him?" asked the bearded man.

"Drag him over to the corner of the building there, and cover him with a tarp," Whipple said. "I'll send word out to the ranch and see if they want to claim his body."

Payson, his gun now back in the holster, bent down to pick up the unbroken bottle of whiskey. Then, without so much as a word, he mounted his horse and rode away. He did not even notice the shining black coach arriving just as he left.

By the time the coach had pulled into the station at Freeland, Amy was ready for the opportunity to walk around and stretch her legs. When she stepped out of the coach, she saw a dozen people gathered around something on the ground near the corner of the building. Curious as to what had attracted so much attention, she walked over to join them.

When she saw what it was, she gasped.

There, lying under a dirty tarpaulin, she saw a body. It

was shrouded from the face down to the knees. The man's feet, covered by badly worn boots, protruded from the bottom of the tarp. One hand, its fingernails dirty and ragged, stuck out from the side, the fingers themselves curled as if grabbing hold of something. A sweat-stained hat lay on the ground nearby.

"My God!" Amy gasped. "What happened to this poor man?"

A thin, dust-covered man standing beside her squirted a stream of tobacco juice from the side of his mouth and then wiped his mustache with the back of his hand. "He got hisself shot," the man said.

"It was the albino that shot 'im," a bearded man added. He, too, was covered with dust, wearing nondescript trousers and a dirty shirt. "Slicker'n a whistle he was, and he was that fast. It was all just a blur."

"It was a fair fight," another bystander put in. "This feller here went for his gun first."

DuMont had come up beside Amy. "Where's the albino now?" he asked.

"He left outta here soon's the smoke cleared. There weren't no reason for him to stay around an' wait on any of this fella's friends."

"Iffen I was a friend of this fella, I'd think twice about tryin' to settle the score," the tobacco chewer said. "I've heerd tell of that albino. He's the fastest there is . . . faster'n Wild Bill Hickok, faster'n Bat Masterson. Faster even than Rufus Butler."

"Ain't nobody faster'n Rufus Butler," the bearded man said.

"I don't know. I'd sure like to see him an' this albino meet. That'd be a fight you could talk to your grandkids about."

Amy felt her knees weaken and her stomach flutter, and she turned to walk away.

DuMont hurried after her and said, "Are you all right, Miss Coaltree?"

"Mr. DuMont, did you hear them talking back there?"

"You mean those men? Did they say something to offend you?"

"They were talking about the shooting as if it were some sort of game," she said. "And yet that poor man is dead."

"I told you this is rough country, Miss Coaltree. That's why your father sent me to escort you."

"Yes," Amy said. "I'm beginning to understand." She took a breath to get hold of herself and get the image of the dead man out of her mind. "Mr. DuMont, I have a confession to make. I've never actually seen my father. We were separated when I was quite young. Would you tell me something about him?"

DuMont laughed. "I guess we're even, Miss Coaltree. I've never seen him either."

"What? But you work for him."

"Your father is a very reclusive man," DuMont explained. "Very few of his employees actually come into personal contact with him. Those of us who communicate directly with him, like myself, receive our instructions by letter."

Amy wondered about the man who was her father. Why was he so secretive? She knew he was an extremely wealthy man. As owner of the Coaltree Cross-country Express Company, he was one of the wealthiest men in America. Is that what great wealth did to a man—make him withdraw from life?

After a stop of a few minutes, the traveling party reboarded the coach to continue their journey. As they left Freeland, Amy glanced back and saw the dead man's body being loaded onto the back of a wagon. An uncontrollable shiver passed through her as she turned again to face the front of the moving stage.

It rained hard in Casper that evening. The dirt streets became quagmires, and even the planks that had been placed across them as walkways at the corners were awash. A lone rider rode down the street, his slicker collar turned up, his hat brim turned down. Water cascaded down his back. The horse's hooves pulled from the mud with loud, sucking sounds, and the animal had its head down in a vain attempt to avoid the rain.

Angus Hightower, standing on the boardwalk, watched the rider as he passed, probably on his way to a nearby ranch. Angus was a large, muscular man with blue eyes, a weathered but unwrinkled face, and brindled hair of dark reddish brown streaked with gray. He was trying to avoid the worst of the rain by keeping as close to the sides of the buildings as he could.

He hurried down the boardwalk toward the welcome dry shelter of the Crystal Palace saloon. In the blacksmith's shop behind him he could hear the ringing sound of steel on steel as Big Troy, the black man who was the local smithy, pounded on the rims that would reband the wheels on a Wyoming Rapid Express stage.

Angus owned that stage, as well as the two other Concord coaches and thirty-six horses that made up the Wyoming Rapid Express. His small stage line was the only connection between Casper and the railroad at Medicine Bow, and that meant it was the only transportation link between Casper and the rest of the world.

Angus had been in Casper for a little over six months now, and in that brief time he had become one of the leading citizens of the community. He did not speak much of his past, but that was not expected of him. When a man moved into a western community, took up honest work, and treated his friends and business associates fairly, he was not asked too many probing questions.

When Angus finally had reached the saloon and entered it, he stood just inside the door and took off his dripping raincoat and hat. The room was aromatic with pipe and cigar tobacco, beer and whiskey. It also served as a restaurant, which accounted for the pleasing odors of cooking meat and vegetables that wafted from the kitchen.

The Crystal Palace was different from most of the other saloons Angus had seen in the small towns of the West. It had a polished mahogany bar with a brass footrail and brass towel rings, from which hung clean, white towels for the customers. In addition to the bar, there were a dozen polished tables for drinking, eating, or playing cards. The walls were covered with white wainscoting halfway up from the floor, and with red, flocked paper above. There was a picture rail around the top of the wall from which hung long wires suspending large paintings—not of reclining nudes, like most saloon paintings, but of pastoral scenes and seascapes.

But the most ornate, most noticeable feature of the saloon was the large crystal chandelier, from which the Crystal Palace took its name. Shipped out from St. Louis, it was the pride of every citizen of Casper. On bright days, when the sun was just right, the glass prisms of the chandelier would catch the sun and neatly separate the light into all the colors of the spectrum, projecting brilliant rainbows onto the bar, tables, walls, floor, and ceiling of the saloon.

The establishment had been conceived of and built after the end of the Civil War by Fort Casper's commander, General Jeremy G. Waddell, and the U.S. Army surgeon there, Dr. James Tice. At first regarded as a gathering place of the military and civilian elite, the Crystal Palace had subsequently gone through a series of unexpected changes to become something quite different.

In 1866, when it had appeared that the transcontinental railroad would be built along the North Platte River, passing through the environs of Fort Casper, there had been a boom time. Furnishings for the Crystal Palace were brought in, and the building was erected. A civilized alternative to run-of-the-mill saloons, it was not only a social club for the officers but quickly became an attraction for travelers, inspiring some to put down roots in the area instead of just passing through. The Carbon County Bank had opened soon afterward, and it had seemed a sure bet that Casper was destined to become a first-class frontier town on the Oregon Trail.

But late the following year, amid all the boom and bustle, the U.S. Army abandoned Fort Casper and moved the military post eastward to Fort Fetterman. An even greater blow to local prosperity was struck when the route of the Union Pacific Railroad was moved south, taking it through Medicine Bow instead of along the North Platte River. This one-two punch brought Casper's rapid growth to a screeching halt, but it also set the stage for the arrival of Marybeth Staley, who bought the Crystal Palace and proceeded to rejuvenate it.

"Angus, what are you doing out there? Don't you have enough sense to get in out of the rain?" Marybeth Staley teased, greeting him at the door of her establishment. A forty-year-old woman, she had hair that was still a vibrant red and a body still lithe and young looking.

Angus Hightower smiled at her. "Well, I'm not made of sugar," he said. "So I'm not likely to melt." He hung his dripping coat and hat on a hook and then took a deep whiff. "What's Jenny cooked up back there tonight? Whatever it is, it smells good, and it's really making me hungry."

Marybeth laughed. "Since when do you need anything to make you hungry? Come on, I waited my supper for you. We can eat together."

Angus was greeted warmly by the other customers as he crossed the floor to the table nearest the piano. There was no such thing as a reserved table at the new Crystal Palace, but every time Angus came into the saloon, he chose this one. In view of his position in the community, and taking into account his personal relationship with the owner of the saloon, the other customers recognized the table as his and never used it.

"Hey, Smith!" someone called. A neat, slender man standing at the bar turned toward the customer who had called his name. In his suit, silk vest, and string tie, he looked a little out of place amidst the coarse trousers and cotton shirts of the patrons.

"Play us somethin', will ya? A little music might keep the wet and gloom out of this place."

"Be glad to," Smith replied, taking his beer with him as he moved toward the piano. He nodded at Angus and Marybeth as he took his seat at the piano, where he daily earned his wages.

"Smith, you want to join us for supper?" Angus invited.

"Thank you, no. I've eaten," Smith answered.

"A piece of cheese and a crust of bread," Marybeth scolded. "Hardly enough to keep you alive."

"It doesn't require much energy to play the piano," Smith said, smiling. It was a pleasant smile, but there was something more to it, a hint of the mystery that always lingered around the piano player. Smith began playing "Buffalo Gals," and the bouncy music brightened the mood, and soon there was laughter and cheery conversation at the bar and all the tables.

Angus liked Smith. He had never met a better-mannered young man, nor one who was more willing to be of service. Angus recalled the night last winter when Smith had ridden through a driving blizzard to take laudanum to a ranch worker. The man had been dying from internal injuries caused by broken ribs, after a horse had kicked him in the chest. Smith had not even known the cowboy, but he had known that the laudanum could ease the pain of the man's last few hours, so he had ridden twelve miles, without complaint, through deep snowdrifts and numbing cold.

Even so, Smith was perceived as something of a dandy and was often teased by the customers. The teasing seldom got out of hand, and on the one or two occasions when it had, Angus had stepped in on Smith's behalf. No one wanted to cross Angus Hightower, and no one really wanted to hurt Smith. He was, after all, their piano player, and no one had ever heard anyone better, so they were eager to keep him around.

"Have you got Big Troy working on the wheels?" Marybeth asked, as they waited for their meal.

"Yes," Angus said. "He said he'd have the coach ready by tomorrow. He's a good man to have around."

"Yes, he is. He reminds me of someone who worked for my father back in Mississippi."

For just a moment, Marybeth's eyes opened like windows to her soul and Angus had a more intimate view of her person than he had ever had before. He felt like an intruder, as if he had accidentally happened onto Marybeth in her bath, and he looked away. Marybeth, realizing she had lost herself in reminiscence, smiled and reached out to put her hand on his.

"Listen to me," she said, "talking about other places and other times when everything I've ever wanted is right here."

It was the closest Marybeth had ever come to articulating her feelings about Angus. Though there was a deep and growing attachment between them, it had until now been largely unspoken. Marybeth was always friendly with her customers; that was one of the reasons the Crystal Palace was so popular. But until Angus had come along, she had never paid more attention to one customer than another. Angus had changed all that. He was special to her, and everyone knew it.

This relationship was a new experience to Angus as well. During his years of bachelorhood he had flirted with saloon girls and dance-hall dollies; he had even been drawn on occasion to the company of a soiled dove. But until he met Marybeth Staley, no woman had ever been more to him than a temporary diversion. Some time ago he had realized that Marybeth was much more important to him than that.

The immediate situation was spared from becoming more awkward by the arrival of Jenny, the waitress, with their supper. Beef and dumplings, green beans, and corn made up the fare, with an extra plate of steaming biscuits, butter, and plum jam thrown in for good measure.

"Ah, Jenny," Angus said, rubbing his hands together in glee. "I've never sat to a more appetizing table."

"Eat it all, Mr. Hightower, but be sure'n save room for the cherry cobbler I got made."

"I'll make room," Angus promised, picking up a fork and starting in.

A cowboy entered the saloon just then, and after reaching out over the swinging doors to pour the rain from the crown of his hat, he walked to the bar to order a drink.

"Still raining, Jimmy?" Fred Stearman, the bartender, greeted him.

"Naw, it's near 'bout stopped," the cowboy answered. He took his drink and then turned around and saw Angus and Marybeth at their supper. "Angus, your afternoon stage is runnin' some late, ain't it?"

"No," Angus answered. "It arrived on time, at two."

"Well, I just seen a stage up on Casper Mountain Road. If it ain't one of your stages, whose is it?"

"I don't have any idea," Angus replied.

Word of the approaching stage circulated through the saloon, and everyone began speculating about who it might be. A few minutes later someone on the porch called out, "It's just comin' across the river now!"

Angus walked over to the door and watched as the coach rolled to a stop in front of the saloon. A gleaming black rig with polished brass lamps and silver scrollwork around the doors, it was pulled by six perfectly matched white horses that were now spattered with mud and steaming from their efforts. They were magnificent animals, and Angus was sure they could pull the stage along at a brisk trot for hours without stopping.

The driver and an immense shotgun guard, still wearing yellow slickers even though the rain had stopped, climbed down. After the driver put a step stool on the ground and opened the door, a handsome man wearing a suit stepped out and then turned back to assist a beautiful dark-haired woman. As he led her into the saloon, those gathered by the door backed out of their way.

The man looked around the room, studying the faces of those who were staring at him.

"Can I help you?" Marybeth asked.

"Are you the proprietress?" the handsome man replied.

"Yes."

"I take it we can get something to eat?"

"Yes, of course," Marybeth said, immediately turning to look at the tables and selecting the best one.

"Mister, you can't get better food in Casper than you can get right here," Fred said proudly.

The man looked at the bartender and then around the saloon with obvious disdain. "Yes, well, I'm sure that would not be difficult elsewhere," he muttered.

After Marybeth had shown the couple to their table, the driver and guard took seats at a table on the opposite side of the room. The man and woman ordered dinner for themselves, the driver, and the shotgun guard.

Other than the extraordinary size of the guard, he and the driver were no different from the hundreds of other men who had come through the saloon. It was the other man and the woman with him who drew the attention, the woman because she was so attractive and well dressed, the man because of his haughty manner and constant complaining. Everyone in the room heard him loudly express his dissatisfaction with the dinner wine.

"What do you mean you don't have Château Lafite-Rothschild?" he demanded of Marybeth. "What type of wine do you have?"

"We have a house red and a house white," Marybeth answered. "A Burgundy and a Chablis."

"Unacceptable, totally unacceptable," the man responded.

"I'll have a glass of Burgundy," the dark-haired woman said, smiling pleasantly.

The wine and meal were served, and though everyone looked toward them with curious glances, no one bothered them during their meal. Marybeth, observing wryly that the man was enjoying the "unacceptable Burgundy," returned to her table and rejoined Angus.

"Who do you think they are?" Marybeth asked.

"I don't know," Angus said. "But from where I sit, it looks like her company would be a lot more pleasant than his."

*   *   *

Smith had stopped playing when the newcomers arrived, and now he studied them over the rim of his glass. He thought he had never seen anyone so beautiful as this young woman.

When the man and woman finished their meal, the man snapped his fingers toward Marybeth.

"I reckon that means for you to run over there," Angus chuckled.

"I'll tell you the truth, sometimes it pains me to be a lady." Marybeth got up and walked over to their table.

"Where might I find the Casper Hotel?" the man asked her.

"This is the Casper Hotel."

"This? This is a saloon."

"And a restaurant and a hotel," Marybeth explained.

"Surely there must be some mistake," the man said to the young woman with him. "Your father can't expect you to stay in a saloon."

"Mister, this is the nicest and cleanest hotel in town," Marybeth protested.

"I am Wesley DuMont," was his indignant reply.

Marybeth looked at him in puzzlement for a moment before saying, "Forgive me, but is that name supposed to mean something to me?"

DuMont cleared his throat. "I happen to be the executive secretary for Ben Coaltree. I suppose you've heard of *him*?"

"Yes, of course I have."

"This," DuMont said, gesturing toward the woman next to him, "is Miss Amy Coaltree, his daughter. Mr. Coaltree has left instructions for me to board her at the Casper Hotel until he arrives."

"Mr. Coaltree is coming here?"

"That is my understanding."

"When?"

"I wasn't told. But that doesn't matter. What does matter is that you provide suitable living quarters for his daughter." DuMont looked around the room and made a face. "Though I doubt that is possible."

Marybeth smiled warmly at Amy. "Miss Coaltree, I'll do the best I can."

"Oh, I'm sure I will like it here, and please, call me Amy. You have a lovely place, Miss . . ."

"Staley. Marybeth Staley, and I would be honored if you called me Marybeth."

"Marybeth. What a lovely name. The chandelier is exquisite. I shall look forward to seeing it lighted up."

"It's about time to light it now," Marybeth said, smiling, and she signaled to Fred. Fred walked over to the wall behind the bar and started turning a crank, which lowered the chandelier.

Angus, who had been watching, had noticed the arrogance and rudeness of the young man with Coaltree's daughter. Rising and walking over to where Marybeth was standing, he asked DuMont, "You work for Ben Coaltree, do you?"

"Yes." DuMont looked Angus over, screwing up his lips as if he had just bitten into a lemon. "Do you know him?"

"We're in the same business," Angus said. "I'm Angus Hightower. I own the stage line that operates between here and Medicine Bow."

"Oh . . . do you, now?" DuMont asked. He smiled thinly. "Then you are just the man I need to see, Mr. Hightower. Coaltree Cross-country Express would like to buy you out. If you would name a price . . ."

"I'm afraid Wyoming Rapid Express is not for sale," Angus said firmly.

"I don't believe you understand. You see, Mr. Coaltree doesn't allow competitors to stay in business very long. If you're smart, you'll sell while the offer is on the table."

"And if I'm not smart?"

"You'll hang on until you start losing so much money that you can't last another day," DuMont said. "Then you'll go broke, and we'll take over the company for peanuts. Nothing personal, you understand, but Coaltree Express Company will win out in the end. We always do."

"We? Tell me, Mr. DuMont, do you own part of the company?"

"Well, no. That is, not exactly." For an instant, as DuMont was put on the defensive, his confidence seemed to falter. But he quickly recovered. "Under the circumstances," he resumed, "Mr. Coaltree coming here and all, I will be taking a personal interest in dismantling your operation."

"I see." Angus had a thoughtful look on his face.

"Please understand me, Mr. Hightower. My tactics will be open and aboveboard. But I *will* succeed."

"Do you enjoy Coaltree's full confidence?" Angus asked.

"Of course. Do you think I could represent him if I did not?"

"I suppose not," Angus said.

"Amy, would you like a closer look at the chandelier?" Marybeth asked when the chandelier had reached its lowest position.

"Yes, thank you." Amy rose and walked over to the chandelier as Fred began replacing the candles that had burned too short.

"It would be wonderful to have a gas chandelier," Marybeth explained, "but I'm afraid Casper lacks that modern convenience."

"Oh, but the gas lights would be much too bright," Amy said. "No, I think the soft lighting of a candle is much more lovely."

"And more trouble," Fred complained, as he cleaned away the wax.

When the candles were replaced, Fred lit all of them and then winched the chandelier back into place. The room was suffused with a soft, golden glow. Considerably more illumination was added as kerosene lamps around the room were lighted.

"Hey, Smith, you just gonna sit there and gawk all day, or are you going to play something for us?" The pointedly good-natured question came from one of the tables near the piano.

"Oh, yes," Amy said to the piano player as she walked toward her table with Marybeth. "Please, do play."

"Would you like anything special, Miss Coaltree?" Smith asked.

"Oh, just anything would be nice," Amy said.

"Yes, don't tax yourself beyond your limit," DuMont said, pitching a coin over to land on the top of Smith's piano. "Just play one of your drinking ditties."

Smith looked at DuMont, and for a moment there was something in Smith's eyes that made DuMont feel a sense of apprehension. He shuddered, and at the same instant he recalled that he and the other boys in the orphanage used to say that such a shudder meant someone had stepped on your grave. But the look in Smith's eyes was gone almost as soon as DuMont had seen it. He was not even sure he had seen it in the first place. He felt a sense of shame over the momentary apprehension, and to cover it, he barked out, "Well, play, man. Play!"

Smith turned back to the piano. He sat at the keyboard for a moment and then began to play. The beautiful notes of Mozart's Sonata in F major filled the room. The music spilled out, a steady, never-wavering string of melodic phrases with a single melody weaving through the piece like a thread of gold woven through the finest cloth. The playing silenced all conversation and stilled the clinking of glasses and bottles.

Amy, startled by the music, looked toward the piano. She had attended concerts in the finest theaters in Europe, but she could honestly say that this man sitting at an upright piano in a saloon in Wyoming was playing as beautifully as anyone she had ever heard. Perhaps it was the moment, the quiet room, the softly lit chandelier, the incongruity of finding such music in a place so far from a cultural center, but Amy had never been moved so deeply by a song before.

When the last note was a lingering echo, the customers in the saloon broke into applause. Amy studied Smith's face, and she could almost see him come back from some place far away. Then Smith stood up and bowed to the customers. The same act by anyone else in such a place would have appeared foolish, a parody, but from Smith it seemed as natural as a handshake.

After the applause and the bow, Smith smiled. He sat back down and began playing a lively rendition of "Cowboy Joe," and the mood was broken.

"Does he often play that kind of music?" Amy asked Marybeth.

"Not as often as I would like," Marybeth said. She smiled. "You should feel honored. I'm sure he played it just for you."

"I am honored," Amy said sincerely, "and touched."

Chapter Three

The audience stood in tribute as their thunderous applause filled the auditorium.

"Monsieur, you have captivated all of us with your playing. You are the sensation of the year. Tomorrow we leave for Vienna, then—"

"I'm afraid there will be no Vienna. Tomorrow I leave for the United States."

"The United States? But I don't understand. The world is your oyster, monsieur. Why would you go back to the United States? They are fighting a war there."

"That's why I must go. My father has called me back. I have an obligation."

"But, no . . . you are beyond such petty squabbles now. You are a man of the world, a true cosmopolitan. What care you of a war between bickering neighbors? I beg of you, monsieur, do not return. Your music is a gift from God. You speak of obligation, and I agree, you do have an obligation. You have a sacred obligation to share your music with the world."

"I'm sorry, Monsieur Mouchette. I must go back."

Smith woke up, and for a moment the feelings of the dream were so vivid that he believed Monsieur Mouchette was there in the room with him. It took a moment for him to realize that he was not in Paris, but in Casper, Wyoming.

Smith got out of bed and walked over to the chiffonier,

where he poured water from the porcelain pitcher into a
basin. He washed his face, lathered his skin with soap,
and began to shave. As he did so, he wondered why he
had dreamed of Paris. He had left Paris over ten years
ago, and a lot had happened since then. Why had that part
of his life suddenly returned to haunt him?

But even as he asked the question, he knew the answer.
It was Amy Coaltree.

Smith believed that he had never seen a more beautiful
young woman than Amy Coaltree. From the moment he
had first seen her, he had been captivated by her.

He finished shaving, wiped the residue of lather from
his face, and then slapped the towel down angrily. What
right had he to be thinking about a young woman like
Amy Coaltree? She was the daughter of one of the wealthiest men in America—and Smith was a saloon piano player.
There once had been a time when she might have found
him acceptable as a suitor, but that had been long ago,
when his name had been on the lips of cultured people
throughout Europe, when newspapers had lavished praise
on him. That had been long ago, indeed.

"Is this really all you want out of life?" his father had
asked him that morning so long ago. "To be a piano
player?"

"Papa, the downstairs dandy in a New Orleans bawdyhouse is a piano player. I intend to be a concert pianist."

"And that's what you want?"

They were standing on a pillared porch in front of the
great, columned mansion that was Rose Hall. His father
was giving him a going-away picnic, and neighbors and
relatives crowded together on the well-kept lawn. Dozens
of house slaves hustled about serving food and drink to the
guests.

"Yes, Papa, it is."

"But to do nothing with your life but make music—
whether in a bawdyhouse or on a concert stage—seems
like such a waste," his father complained.

"Is it a waste to want to do something to make the world a little more beautiful? When you went to Richmond last year, didn't you bring back two new paintings?"

"Yes, but that's different."

"Why is it different? You bought the paintings because they are a part of the life you have made for us. Papa, I believe man was meant for more than mere survival, and you have raised me to believe that. Thanks to you I've been surrounded by elegance and beautiful things."

"It isn't entirely thanks to me. You owe a big thanks to cotton and to the money Rose Hall makes."

"Well, then, consider Rose Hall. This house is as beautiful as a Greek temple. Why do we live in such a mansion when a simple log cabin would protect us from the elements?"

"There's more to a home than a place to get out of the rain. There's—"

"Beauty?"

"Beauty, yes." He paused for a long moment. "I . . . all right, I see what you mean."

"Papa, I want to give some beauty back to the world, and I know I can do it with my music. I've gone as far as I can go with the teachers in this country. Franz Liszt is the finest teacher in the world, and he has accepted me. I can't pass up an opportunity to study under him."

His father smiled. "All right, go to Europe! You'll get no further argument from me. Besides, I must confess that I remember my own tour of Europe with great fondness. I wasn't married to your mother then, of course, and the girls of Paris . . . Oh, well!" His eyes sparkled. "Some things are better left unsaid." He held up his glass. "If a concert pianist is what you want to be, son, then I want you to be the best."

Smith looked at his reflection in the mirror of his small room over the Crystal Palace.

"A concert pianist, Papa? The piano players in the New Orleans bawdyhouses are miles closer to that than I am now."

At that moment Smith heard two pistol shots in the street below. It was too early for a drunk to be celebrating, but the shots did not have the urgency that denoted shots fired in anger. He walked over to the window to see what was going on.

Wes DuMont had the special coach pulled to the center of the street. All of the mud and dirt from its journey the day before had been scrubbed off, and the coach glistened brightly in the morning sun. The six perfectly matched white horses stood in well-mannered, well-groomed silence. Simmons, the driver, stood in liveried splendor, holding his hand on the halter of the first horse.

Wes DuMont had fired the pistol shots in order to attract attention. His ploy had worked; several of the townspeople were beginning to gather around the stage.

DuMont climbed up onto the driver's box so he could address the assembled spectators. "Ladies and gentlemen," he said, "allow me to introduce myself. I am Wes DuMont, executive secretary to Mr. Ben Coaltree, owner of the Coaltree Cross-country Express Company. I am pleased to say that, in Mr. Coaltree's name, I hereby announce the start of a new stagecoach service. Beginning tomorrow, Coaltree Cross-country Express Company will have morning and afternoon departures for Medicine Bow, as well as two return trips from Medicine Bow."

Angus Hightower, who had heard the gunshots and seen the coach drawn to the middle of the street, had come over to see what was going on. He was standing in the crowd with the others. DuMont's announcement did not surprise him, since DuMont had already told him that he intended to start a stage line to put Wyoming Rapid Express out of business.

"We got a stage line, mister," someone called.

"Yeah, an' it's servin' us real good. What makes you think we'd want to change?"

DuMont smiled and then motioned to the giant, who was standing beside the coach. "Mr. Meeker, would you open the door to the coach, please?"

Meeker opened the door, revealing the deep, rich red interior of the coach, and there were a few *oohs* and *ahs* over the beauty of it.

"Of course, the inside of the coach is pleasing to the eye, but notice, if you will, the fine soft leather on the thickly padded seats. We've spared no effort, not only in pleasing our passengers aesthetically, but in making them comfortable as well. In addition to the cushioned luxury seats, the leather padding extends up the sides and onto the doors of the coach, thus protecting the passengers from injury during any abrupt tossing about, should the coach traverse a hole in the road. However, this coach is so beautifully suspended on the finest thoroughbraces, that such an event is unlikely. I can personally assure you that riding in it is like riding on a cloud. I shall have four coaches on this run, all four as elegantly appointed as this coach and pulled by stock as fine as these animals."

Those who were gathered around the coach looked inside and then moved away so the others could get a close-up look as well. Angus stepped up to the coach, and even he had to admit that as far as luxurious accommodations were concerned, his coaches could not complete with this elegant vehicle.

"This is a fine coach all right," one of the spectators said. "And I ain't never seen no better horses than them you got hooked up. But, mister, what kind of customers you think you got here? We're farmers and ranchers, or merchants, just regular people tryin' to make ends meet. We can't afford to ride around like the king of Prussia."

His comment was seconded by half a dozen other people.

DuMont smiled broadly. "Ah, so you're worried about cost, are you, my good man? Well, I don't blame you. When you see a coach as luxurious as this, you are sure to think you can't afford it. But the cost for a round-trip ticket to Medicine Bow will be but three dollars."

"Three dollars? That's ridiculous!" Angus spurted. "You can't even break even at that price! Especially with equipment and stock like this."

"Nevertheless, that's our price," DuMont said smugly.

"How are you going to deal with that, Angus?" someone asked. "You going to lower your price to match theirs?"

"I guess I have no choice," Angus replied. "Folks, my coaches aren't as elegant as this one, but my prices will be the same. And my drivers have been making this run for two years, so you'll have experience on your side."

"Experience," someone said. "Who cares about experience when you can ride in something like this?" He ran his hand across the shining lacquer finish. "Just once, I'd like to feel like a rich man, and ridin' in somethin' like this could do it for me."

"I don't know," someone else said. "I never trusted somethin' all painted up pretty like that. It's like maybe they're tryin' to cover up somethin'. No, sir, Angus's coaches have done me good enough for these past six months. I reckon I'll keep on ridin' with him."

"Thanks, Porter," Angus said.

"Me, I'm gonna spread it around," someone else put in. "One time I'll go with Angus, another time I might use this here coach."

While this was going on in the street, Smith, now dressed for the day, was just coming downstairs in the Crystal Palace. He saw Amy Coaltree sitting at a table and having her breakfast.

"Oh, Mr. Smith," she said. "Won't you join me for breakfast?"

"I never eat breakfast," Smith replied. "But I'll have a cup of coffee if you don't mind the company."

Amy signaled Jenny, who brought the coffeepot over to fill a cup for Smith.

"I didn't get a chance to tell you last night how much I appreciated your beautiful playing."

"Thank you."

"I must confess that I was very surprised to hear such music."

"You mean you were surprised that I could play something more than drinking ditties?" Smith asked.

Amy flushed red and then smiled an embarrassed smile. "Mr. DuMont was rude to say such a thing," she said. "And, no, that's not what I meant. What I meant was, one doesn't expect to find a pianist of your caliber in such a place."

"I understand. I sometimes wonder myself what I'm doing in such a place."

"What *are* you doing here?"

"What are *you* doing here?" Smith countered. "I find it a stranger circumstance that the daughter of the wealthiest man in America should be here."

"Well, the answer to that question is quite simple," Amy said. "I'm here to see my father."

Smith smiled broadly. "And I guess that's the strangest part of it—that a man as wealthy as your father would arrange to meet you here. What's he like?"

"Now I'm afraid it's my time to be mysterious. I can't answer that. You see, I've never met him. I was only a baby when my mother took me back to Boston."

"Why have you come to see him now?"

"My mother died just this year. I've always been curious about my father, so I wrote him and asked if he would mind a visit from me."

"I hope he doesn't disappoint you."

"Thank you. I hope he doesn't either. Mr. Smith . . ."

"Why don't you drop the mister, and just call me Smith?"

"No first name?"

"I never use it."

"All right, Smith. Tell me if I'm wrong, but I would be willing to bet that you have played piano on the stage somewhere. Perhaps back east?"

"Yes," Smith said.

"I can't believe that it wasn't a successful tour. You are much too talented for that. And yet you are here. Why?"

"Maybe I like it out here."

Amy smiled broadly. "Well, I can understand that. A couple of ladies I met on the train on the way out complained most bitterly about the scenery, but I found it breathtaking. The people have been nice, too. There's only been one thing to mar my trip thus far."

"What was that?"

"Yesterday morning we stopped in a place called Freeland. It was just a stagecoach stop, really. No town that I could see."

"Yes, it's a way station."

"My attention was drawn to something on the ground, and when I walked over to see what it was, I saw a man's body, lying under a canvas cover. He had been killed, shot down, they said, in a gun duel."

"That happens out here more than anyone would like to admit," Smith said. "Did anyone say what happened?"

"As near as I could understand, the episode took place over a bottle of whiskey. Imagine, getting killed for a bottle of whiskey. I found the entire thing quite disconcerting."

"Who was killed?"

"I don't know. They said it was a cowboy who worked nearby. No one spoke much of him, but they were quite interested in the man who shot him."

"Who did shoot him?"

"I don't recall if they actually mentioned a name," Amy said. "But someone called him an albino."

"Payson," Smith said. "Sometimes called Fast Charlie Payson."

"Do you *know* this Payson person?"

"Only by reputation. He's very fast with a gun."

"Yes, that's what they all said. They say Mr. Payson is supposed to be faster than anyone else. They mentioned some other names as well, but the only name I remember is someone by the name of Rufus Butler. And one of the most troubling aspects, Smith, is that they were all talking about it as if it were some sort of contest."

"In a way, I suppose it is," Smith said. "A contest to see who lives and who dies."

Amy shivered. "I must say, this is not a part of the West that I enjoy."

"Nevertheless, it is a part of the West, and if you are going to accept any of it, you must accept all of it."

"Why? You certainly haven't accepted it."

"What do you mean?"

"All the other men I've seen out here wear guns in holsters, or stuck down in their belts or in their pockets. You don't wear a gun. Instead of bringing violence to this country, you bring beauty. Why, you're a one-man crusade."

"Don't make me into something I'm not," Smith said uncomfortably.

"You're just being modest."

Marybeth had been standing in the door, looking out into the street, watching DuMont make his pitch. She walked back near their table, and at Amy's invitation sat with them.

"I was just telling Smith how much I loved his music," Amy commented.

"I agree," Marybeth said. "Everyone loves Smith's music. But I'm afraid it's going to be difficult for me to like your friend Mr. DuMont," she admitted.

"He isn't my friend, actually. He's an employee of my father's. I met him yesterday morning when he arranged to escort me from Medicine Bow to Casper. But I wish you wouldn't be so quick to judge him. I haven't found him to be unmannerly in any way."

"I'm certain his manners are fine," Marybeth said. "It's what he's doing right now that I don't like."

"What is he doing out there?" Smith asked.

"Mr. DuMont is soliciting customers for a new stage-coach line. He's cut the round-trip price from here to Medicine Bow to three dollars."

"Three dollars?" Smith said in disbelief.

"I don't understand. Why wouldn't you like that?" Amy asked. "That's a good deal for the passengers, isn't it?"

"No," Smith said. "It's a terrible deal."

"Oh, I know you are concerned with the stage line Mr. Hightower owns, but you must admit that the people of Casper stand only to gain from good, healthy competition."

"Miss Coaltree," Smith started.

"Please, call me Amy."

"Amy, there is nothing healthy about this competition. Don't you know how these things work?"

"I guess not."

"It's very simple," Smith explained. "First Coaltree Cross-country Express comes into a location where another stage line is operating. Next, they cut the fare in half. The competition usually can't meet that price and soon goes under. Then, as soon as Coaltree Cross-country has control of the route, they jack the prices back up to twice what they were originally. After that, they replace these elegant coaches, probably with equipment they'll buy from Angus after he's bankrupt. Finally, they'll cut the service in half."

"Oh," Amy said. "I . . . I didn't know."

"You're being a little hard on her, aren't you, Smith? After all, it's her father who does such things, not her."

"Or in this case, Mr. DuMont," Amy said.

"But he's speaking for your father."

"Yes, I suppose he is," Amy agreed. "I hadn't realized my father was such a bad man."

"No one is saying your father is a bad man, honey," Marybeth said, putting her hand on that of the younger woman. "He's just a hard businessman, that's all. And sometimes when a person does hard business, other people get hurt. In this case, the one who will be hurt most is Angus Hightower."

"Is Mr. Hightower your beau?" Amy asked innocently.

Marybeth laughed, and a touch of color flamed her cheeks.

"What about it, Marybeth?" Smith teased. "Is he your beau?"

"Let's just say that Angus and I are very good friends," Marybeth said.

Suddenly they heard a loud commotion and several excited voices in the street.

"What is it? What's going on?" Amy asked.

They all got up from the table and hurried to the door to look outside, where they saw a black man, almost as big and powerfully built as Meeker, running down the street.

"It's Big Troy," Marybeth said.

The big man began shouting, "Fire! Fire! Come quick, my shed is on fire!"

"Oh, Smith, help them!" Marybeth said, but she need not have spoken, because Smith was already out the door.

Big Troy's shout galvanized Smith and everyone else into action, and there was a rush toward the blacksmith's shop, where smoke was already billowing out into the street.

"We can save the shed if we hurry," Big Troy said. "But it's Mista Angus's stage what's in the most danger!"

Angus, who had come running with everyone else, groaned as he remembered that he had left one of his stages with Big Troy so the blacksmith could reband the wheels.

It was not only the people who were standing around listening to DuMont who hurried to the blacksmith shed; buildings on both sides of the street emptied as people rushed to fight the fire.

When he got there, Smith noticed that the shed itself was not on fire. The only thing in flames was the coach, and it was burning furiously.

"Grab the coach tongue," Smith shouted.

Half a dozen men grabbed the tongue and pulled the coach out of the shed into the middle of the street. Once there, the men joined a bucket brigade that was forming, helping to pass buckets from nearby water troughs to the men closest to the stage, who then splashed the water onto the fire. They finally doused the flames, but by then there was nothing left but the charred frame and blackened wheels of what had once been a rugged Concord coach.

The big blacksmith was a picture of remorse as he said to the owner of the coach, "Mista Angus, I swears to you, I ain't got no idea how this here happen'. I lef' my shed for a minute, only just a minute, an' when I come back, the coach was on fire."

"Perhaps you should have checked your forge," DuMont said. Unlike the others, he had not rushed to the site of the fire, but now sauntered up to the crowd around it. "I know it's sometimes difficult for you people to think about things like that, but—"

"What do you mean by 'you people'?" Angus asked pointedly.

"Well, I mean he's a colored man. Sometimes colored folk get confused, that's all," DuMont said.

"Mista Angus, you can look at my forge iffen you want," Big Troy said. "It's stone cold, 'cause I ain't had no fire in it this livelong day. That's why I ain't got no idea how the coach come to catch like it done."

"Big Troy, don't you worry about it any," Angus said. "No one's blaming you."

"No, suh. But I just want you to know how powerful sorry I is that this here happened. An' it happened in my shed, an' that makes it worse."

"If you make a practice of being this careless, I shall certainly think twice before committing one of my stages to you for repair," DuMont said.

"Beggin' your pardon, suh, but iffen you is goin' in business against Mista Angus, I don' reckon I'd be wantin' to work on your coaches anyhow. Mista Angus has been a loyal customer all the while. He's the one brought us a stage line here in the first place, an' it wouldn't seem right for me to work on coaches for his competition."

"You're a rather uppity colored man, aren't you?" DuMont asked.

"Yes, suh, I reckon I is."

During all this, Angus was standing with his hands on his hips, looking at the smoking ruins of his coach. It was a total loss. He realized that he now had only two coaches to compete with the Coaltree Cross-country Express Company's four.

DuMont walked over to stand beside him.

"I must say I don't care much for the blacksmith," DuMont said. "I know the colored people aren't slaves anymore, but that doesn't mean they should forget their place." He clucked his tongue and shook his head. "There's certainly nothing you can do with this, is there?"

"I'm afraid not," Angus said. "I don't know if I'll even be able to salvage any spare parts."

"This loss is going to be hard on you, isn't it?"

"It isn't going to be easy," Angus admitted.

"Yes, well, it's too bad." DuMont declared. "You should've taken Mr. Coaltree's offer. If you had, this would've been his loss, instead of yours."

"Yeah," Angus said. He sighed. "I guess so."

Smith put down his bucket and wiped some soot off his face. He looked over at Meeker, the big bodyguard. Meeker was standing in the street not far from the shed, looking fixedly at Big Troy. The two men were about the same size, though Meeker might have been a little taller. Meeker, Smith noticed, had not helped fight the fire.

It was obvious to Smith that this fire had not happened by accident. The forge was cold, and there were no lighted lanterns in the building. But who could have set the fire? The obvious suspect was DuMont, since he had the most to gain by destroying Hightower's coach. But DuMont, Meeker, and Simmons had all been standing in the middle of the street in plain sight of a hundred or so citizens when the fire had broken out. There could be no better alibi than that.

Smith caught a glimpse of something out of the corner of his eye, and he looked over toward the alley behind the blacksmith's shed. There he saw a man standing quietly, just watching the scene. Though not an old man, the onlooker's hair and eyebrows were snow-white. His skin was pale, his eyes a translucent pink, and he wore a six-gun strapped low on his right hip. Though Smith had never met him, he knew immediately that this was the albino gunfighter, Charlie Payson.

Smith made a mental note that, like Meeker, Payson had watched the townspeople fight the fire, making no effort to help.

Because there was nothing else he could do with his burned-out coach, Angus Hightower had it pulled back into Big Troy's shed. Throughout the day Big Troy salvaged what he could, mostly steel hardware, and disposed of the rest. By late afternoon, there was a huge pile of bolts, nuts, and pins on a bench as Big Troy continued to extract parts from the charred remains.

On the wall above the bench was a faded poster, a drawing of a large black man, his fists poised before him. Below the illustration was an announcement printed in large capital letters:

BIG TROY LUCAS
COLORED BAREFISTED CHAMPION
WILL FIGHT ALL COMERS
FIVE DOLLARS TO THE MAN WHO STAYS IN
THE RING WITH HIM FOR THREE ROUNDS

After Big Troy had removed all the hardware, he prepared to lift the coach body off the burned-out throughbraces. Even though it had been reduced by the fire, the coach body still weighed a little over six hundred pounds, and Big Troy was looking around for a long pole he could use as a lever.

"So . . . you are the colored champion."

Startled by the unexpected voice, Big Troy looked toward his front door. A huge man blocked out the light, and because he was backlit by the setting sun, Big Troy thought for a moment that the visitor might be colored as well. When the visitor stepped inside, however, Big Troy saw that it was John Meeker.

"Good evenin', Mr. Meeker," Big Troy said. He wiped his hands on a rag and nodded toward the poster. "I don't reckon that be true anymore. I got me some age on now, and I expects some of those big bucks comin' outta the South could handle me real good."

"Still, there was the time when we both had a title," Meeker said, looking at the poster.

"Yes, suh, I reckon there was."

"I seem to recall you wanted to fight me then," Meeker said.

"Yes, suh, I reckon I did." Big Troy was carefully sizing up Meeker as they spoke.

Meeker ran his finger over the drawing of a younger, slimmer Big Troy; then he smiled. He still had all of his front teeth, Big Troy noted. That was as good an indication as anything to show how good a fighter Meeker had been. Big Troy could not make the same claim. He was missing two front teeth from the top and two from the bottom.

"Too bad it didn't happen," Meeker said. "It would have been quite a fight."

"I expects so."

Meeker pointed to the coach body. "You want to lift that off?"

"Yes, suh."

Meeker smiled. "You get one end; I'll get the other."

Big Troy returned Meeker's smile and moved into position. Several Casper citizens walking by a moment later gasped and stared at the sight of an entire coach body being carried out the door of the blacksmith's shop by the two powerful men.

Chapter Four

Normally, Amy was not a person who got up at five-thirty in the morning. However, because her room fronted the street, she was awakened the next morning at that early hour by the sound of luggage being loaded onto a coach. She walked over to the window and looked outside. In the gray morning light she could see a stagecoach in front of the Crystal Palace. It was not as elegant or beautiful as the one she had ridden in the day before yesterday, but it was obviously well maintained, with a look of ruggedness about it that inspired confidence.

A young man, Amy guessed about seventeen or eighteen years old, stood on top of the stage, while a middle-aged man handed luggage up to him.

"Billy, put this here'n up front and tie it down so's it don't bounce around none."

"You tellin' me how to do my job, Deekus?" Billy called back down. "I been ridin' shotgun for you for six months now. I reckon I've learned some as to what this here job's about."

Deekus grunted a laugh and then spit out a chew of tobacco and wiped the back of his hand across his mustache. "You signed on thinkin' you'd be blastin' away outlaws and injuns with your fancy shootin'," he said. "You found out ridin' shotgun is some different from what you thought, didn't you?"

"I sure didn't think I'd be loadin' and unloadin' trunks and boxes all day long," Billy growled. He put the box where Deekus told him and then raised up and took his hat off to expose a head of blond hair. "I reckon I'm only gonna do this another few months, though; then I'm gonna get me a job where's there's some excitement."

Amy started to go back to bed. Then she heard Deekus ask, "What do you think, Smith? Can you think of a job excitin' enough for this young firebrand?"

Hearing Smith's name called, Amy hurried back to the window and looked down on the street. She could not see Smith, but she heard his voice from under the porch roof overhang.

"How much more excitement does he want?" Smith teased. "He's got travel and adventure now."

Billy laughed. "Yeah, travel. I get to see Medicine Bow every day."

"That's travel enough, ain't it?" Deekus asked. "That's all the baggage. Come on down, and I'll buy you some breakfast."

"Big deal," Billy said. "Angus pays for our eats when we're workin'."

"Well, then, me and Smith'll let you keep us company. That ought to be worth somethin'," Deekus said good-humoredly.

Amy wondered why Smith was standing out there. Was he leaving on this stage? She hoped not. She had just met him, and she would hate to see him leave so quickly. She told herself she wanted him to stay because she did not want to lose the opportunity to hear him play again, and there was a great deal of truth to that. But there was another reason as well. She had not admitted it to herself—perhaps she had not even recognized it yet—but she was strongly attracted to him.

On impulse, she dressed to go down to breakfast. If he was leaving, she at least wanted to be able to tell him good-bye.

"My goodness," Marybeth said a few minutes later when she saw Amy come down the stairs and walk into the dining room. "What on earth are you doing up so early?"

"I often wake up early," Amy fibbed, not wanting to admit that the real reason she was down here was to see Smith. "I could smell the bacon cooking, and it made me hungry for an early breakfast."

"Well, I have only two tables set," Marybeth said. "One's for the stage driver and shotgun guard, and the other's for the passengers, but you're certainly welcome to join either one you want."

"Thank you," Amy said. She looked toward the two tables and saw Smith sitting with Deekus and Billy. Though not eating, he was drinking a cup of coffee. At the passenger table she saw a young mother with a boy and girl, the boy about six, the girl perhaps four years old. At the same table sat a fat drummer in a gray suit and vest, and an older woman dressed all in black.

"I'll sit over there, if it's all right," Amy said, pointing toward Smith.

"You just go right ahead, honey. I'll send your breakfast out to you," Marybeth said.

All three men stood when Amy joined them, and Smith made the introductions. "Deekus, Billy, this is Miss Amy Coaltree."

The driver just nodded, but Billy brushed his hair back and smiled broadly.

"Deekus is a real western pioneer," Smith explained. "He's driven stagecoaches, hunted buffalo for the railroad, and headed up a wagon train. I guess he's done about everything. He's the driver, and Billy's the shotgun guard."

"That's an awfully important job for someone so young, isn't it?" she said to Billy.

"I'm eighteen," he said defensively. "Eighteen's not all that young. Besides, I'm just about the best shot there is."

"He *is* a very good shot," Smith admitted. "He gave the town a demonstration last year on the Fourth of July."

"I'm going to do it this year, too," Billy boasted. "I'll do a special trick for you."

"I shall look forward to seeing it," Amy said, and Billy beamed under her interest. She looked at Smith. "Are you going somewhere?"

"Me? No," Smith said.

"Oh. When I looked out the window and saw you I thought . . ." Amy let the words die in her throat. She had not intended to let him know she was that interested in what he was doing. It was too late, though, she realized as she saw his satisfied smile. Now he knew she was interested in him, and his smile told her that he returned the interest. The situation was prevented from getting awkward, however, when Marybeth appeared with Amy's breakfast. She also refilled Smith's coffee cup.

"Don't you ever eat anything?" Amy asked Smith.

"Sure."

"I've been here two days and I haven't see you eat a bite."

"Tell you what. What if I have Marybeth fix us a picnic lunch? I could rent a buckboard and show you around. We could picnic out on Bullhead Mesa."

"Oh, that sounds wonderful," Amy said. "I'd love to."

"Be ready by eleven," Smith said.

Amy finished her breakfast and then went out onto the porch to watch the stage leave. While they were at breakfast, the Coaltree Cross-country stage had drawn up behind them. The driver and shotgun guard on the Coaltree stage were new, and as Deekus exchanged a few pleasantries with them, he learned that DuMont had hired several men the day before as drivers, guards, hostlers, and ticket agents. For now they were operating out of a feed store, but plans were already under way to build a stage depot, complete with a place to eat and overnight accommodations for passengers. The Coaltree coach would not be leaving until eight o'clock, the hope being that such a reasonable departure hour would be more attractive to the passengers. With four stages, DuMont had a great deal of flexibility in his schedule.

Angus had no flexibility at all. In order to have two departures and two arrivals per day, one stage had to leave Casper at six A.M., while another stage left Medicine

Bow at the same time. The six A.M. stage from Medicine Bow would turn right around, departing from Casper at two P.M., while the other coach would turn around at Medicine Bow at approximately the same time. Both stages would complete their trips at ten P.M., covering the last part of the run in the dark.

Angus was standing out front, watching the passengers board his stage, when he saw Smith and Amy come out of the Crystal Palace. He moved over to stand beside them.

"Good morning, Mr. Hightower," Amy said brightly.

"Mornin', miss. What gets you out so early?"

"I wanted to watch the excitement," Amy said, indicating the stage that was about to depart.

"Yeah, well, I guess we better watch it while we can. If DuMont does what he says he's going to, I don't know if I can hold on."

"Maybe when my father gets here I can talk to him, tell him to stop," Amy offered.

"Do you think he'd listen to you?" Smith asked.

"I don't know," Amy admitted. "I really have no right to ask such a thing of him. I guess we'll have to wait and see if he accepts me."

"In the brief time I've known you, Amy, I've come to believe your father'd have to be a complete fool not to accept you," Angus said. "And whatever he is, we can assume he isn't a fool."

"Why, thank you," Amy said.

With the four passengers aboard, Deekus let out a whistle and then snapped his long whip over the heads of the team. Under the driver's urging, the horses swung the stage around and trotted briskly down the main street of the town, heading for the river and then Casper Mountain pass. As soon as the stage crossed the river, those who had watched its departure turned to attend to other tasks. Amy, because she was up much earlier than usual, decided to go back to her room and nap for a while. She was asleep when the Coaltree stage left at eight o'clock, carrying only two passengers.

*   *   *

Amy napped for only a short time. She got up again around nine o'clock and took a walk through the town, up one side of the street and down the other. Though the train that brought her west had passed through several little towns, Casper was the first one she had been able to see up close, and she was fascinated by it. Going into the general store, she saw that it was surprisingly well stocked with everything from foodstuffs to hardware. She also browsed through the emporium that was next door, and it seemed to Amy that between these two stores one would be able to purchase all of the essentials for running a household. The bank, with a columned façade and several offices on the second floor, was the most prominent building in town besides the Crystal Palace. Next to the bank was the telegraph office, with a small regional newspaper bureau adjacent to it. Toward the end of the street were the sheriff's office and local jail, a feed store, and a saddle shop, which boasted an extensive array of leather goods for sale. Near the blacksmith's shop Amy noticed, no surprise to her by now, a gunsmith's shop. Besides several boardinghouses, the other establishments seemed to be saloons, though none was in the same class as the Crystal Palace.

It was almost eleven o'clock by the time Amy returned to the Crystal Palace. She had planned to go up to her room until Smith called for her, but she saw Angus and Marybeth sitting at the table near the piano, and at their invitation she joined them.

Angus handed her a yellow envelope, saying, "This telegram came for you this morning."

"Oh, it's from my father," Amy said happily. As she read it, though, her smile faded.

"What is it? Anything wrong?" Marybeth asked.

"No, not really," Amy replied. "It's just that unexpected business has delayed my father. He won't be here for another couple of weeks."

"Oh, I'm sorry," Marybeth said.

Amy smiled. "It's all right. I must say I really am enjoying it here. The only thing that disappoints me is that it will be that much longer before I can talk to him about your situation, Mr. Hightower," Amy said.

Angus smiled and patted her hand affectionately. "Don't you worry about me, Amy. I'll get along just fine."

"But if my father runs you out of business, I'd feel just awful," Amy protested.

"Why don't we talk about something else?" Angus rejoined. "Marybeth tells me you're going on a picnic with Smith."

"Yes," Amy answered. "He's going to show me Bullhead Mesa."

"It's pretty out there," Angus said. "I think you'll like it."

Some men at a nearby table had been talking, and the conversation had been getting louder until it was now on the verge of erupting into a full-scale argument.

"He is *too* faster," one of the men said.

"How do you know? They ain't never gone up against each another, and there ain't no way you can say who's the fastest till they do."

"Well, my cousin, he seen 'em both. He seen the albino gun down a man in Julesburg, and he seen Rufus Butler in a fight back in Dodge. He says the albino's faster."

Smith came down the stairs then, and for the first time Amy saw him wearing something other than a suit and vest. He was wearing denim trousers and a bright yellow cotton shirt. He was handsome in his suit, but she liked him this way, too. Dressed like this, he seemed more a part of the West.

"Ask Smith," one of the arguing men said.

"How would he know?"

"Saloon piano players know more'n you think. They generally keep their eyes open and their mouths shut. That way they learn stuff. Smith, if Rufus Butler was to go against Fast Charlie Payson, who do you think would win?"

"I have no idea," Smith replied.

"It's simple enough," the other man challenged. "The albino is faster, so he'd gun down Butler."

"It doesn't matter who's the fastest," Smith said.

"What do you mean it don't matter who's the fastest?"

"There are other things involved," Smith said.

"Ah, what do you know about it, anyway? You ain't nothin' but a piano player."

"A minute ago you was tellin' me how much piano players was s'posed to know," the partner said.

As neither man was willing to concede his point, the two men abandoned the discussion, and their conversation grew quieter as it drifted onto other subjects.

"I'll tell you who I would want to win," Angus said.

"Who?" Smith asked, looking at him.

"I'd want Rufus Butler to win."

"Why?" Amy asked. "What makes him any better than any other gunfighter?"

"Well, I haven't ever seen Rufus Butler, but they say he never fought or killed unless he was forced into it. They say he didn't like it."

"You're talking of him in the past tense," Amy said. "Is he dead?"

"Nobody knows," Angus replied. "He disappeared right after he killed a ten-year-old kid, a boy in a little cow town in West Kansas."

"A ten-year-old child? So much for Mr. Butler's good nature," Amy said.

"It was an accident," Angus explained. "Everyone who witnessed it agreed on that. But anyway, Butler rode out of that town, and no one has ever seen or heard of him since."

"I heard he was out in California," one of the men at the other table said, rejoining the conversation.

"Harley Mack said he seen in the Denver paper that Butler got hisself kilt by the New York police," the other put in.

"Wherever he is," Angus said, "he's been there for more than two years."

"Well, there you have it," Smith added. "All this talk about who would kill whom if Butler and Payson fought is a waste of energy. Since Butler is nowhere around, there won't be a fight."

"Pity," one of the other men said. "It'd be a dandy."

"A dandy?" Smith challenged. "One of them would end up dead."

"I don't expect a piano-playin' dude like you to understand."

Smith's eyes flashed like a glint of firelight on steel, but Marybeth put her hand on his and said, "Smith, your picnic basket is ready. Why don't you take Amy with you and have a good time?"

"I'm ready if you are," Amy put in quickly.

The steely fire in his eye instantly faded as Smith turned to her and smiled. "Ready?" he said. "I've been ready since this morning. Let's go."

Smith rented a buckboard from the livery stable and drove to Bullhead Mesa. The drive took about an hour, but it passed quickly as Smith pointed out features of interest to Amy. By the time they reached their destination, Amy realized that she was hungry, and she looked forward with eager anticipation to opening the picnic hamper Marybeth had prepared for them.

"Ah, let's see what we have here," Smith said as he spread the red tablecloth across a flat rock and began taking out items. "Uhmm, cold chicken, roast beef, potato salad, sliced cucumbers, baked bread, and a whole cake. Just as I suspected," Smith said, smacking his lips. "She prepared a small banquet for us."

"Oh, my, she doesn't expect us to eat it all, does she? I mean, no more than you eat, how can we possibly do justice to such a meal?"

"Maybe I eat like a camel drinks," Smith teased. "I don't eat often, but when I do eat, I eat a lot." Smith found two glasses and a bottle of wine in the basket. Château Lafite-Rothschild.

Amy read the label and then chuckled. "Poor Wes," she

said. "He wanted a Château Lafite-Rothschild so badly the other night."

Smith smiled. "I'm sure it's one of Marybeth's little jokes." He opened the wine and poured them each a glass.

"Oh, thank you," Amy said. She took a swallow of wine and looked out across the valley. The field before them waved with flowers of every hue and description. Most noticeable among them were white and yellow oxeye daisies, slender white-and-blue columbines, and brilliant red Indian paintbrushes. Beyond the valley, a great range of snowcapped mountains rose.

"I can't get over how incredibly beautiful it is out here," she said, her voice soft with awe.

"And I can't get over how incredibly beautiful you are," Smith replied.

As Amy looked into Smith's eyes, she was frightened by the light of desire she saw there. Her fear was not of Smith alone, though. She was just as frightened of herself, for she knew that her own eyes reflected a hunger every bit as intense as that shown by Smith.

He moved toward her, and as his lips pressed against hers, her head started spinning. For a moment she thought she should protest, but all struggle was impossible. Her blood felt the effects of the wine, and her body warmed with a passionate heat she had never before experienced. The kiss went on, longer than she had ever imagined such a thing could last, and her head grew so light that she abandoned all thought. Finally, Smith broke off the kiss, and Amy was left standing there as limp as a rag doll.

"I'm sorry . . . I'm sorry," Smith said. "I had no right."

"No," Amy said breathlessly. "Don't be sorry. You did not force yourself on me." She looked at the picnic basket and then forced a smile, hoping that her real hunger did not show through. "But I really think we should eat now, don't you? I'm famished."

*   *   *

There was no repeat of the kiss, nor did they speak of it again. Instead they concentrated on other things. They watched prairie dogs cavorting about in the near distance and hawks soaring far above. They imagined all manner of different figures in the clouds and laughed when they found one that looked like Angus. And Smith proved to have a voracious appetite after all. Finally, with the meal eaten and the sun three-quarters of the way through its day's travel, Smith said it was time to start back.

They were about halfway back to Casper when a rider suddenly appeared alongside their buckboard. Amy looked toward him and then, her breath catching in fear, grabbed Smith's arm.

"Smith!" she said. "It's—"

"I know," Smith said quietly. "It's Payson."

Amy felt her heart pounding furiously as the albino rode alongside them. She was terrified as she recalled what she had seen and heard at Freeland, and she was afraid that, at any moment, he might pull his pistol and start shooting away at them.

Payson never said a word, but he looked at Smith in such a way that Amy felt as if he were studying him. His interest in Smith frightened her, because it seemed to be more than a casual curiosity. She tried not to look directly at him. It was not just his being an albino that frightened her; the fact that he was a killer made those terrible, pink-venomed eyes even more terrifying to behold.

Payson was a man whose continued existence depended upon his ability to use and interpret all of his sharpened senses. He survived by knowing instinctively where danger might be. He had never met the man sitting next to the woman in the wagon, yet there was something about him that made Payson uneasy, something that triggered an alarm in the back of his mind.

What was it? Why was he uneasy around this dandy?

Payson continued to ride alongside the buckboard, hoping he would come up with an answer. The woman was clearly terrified. Maybe to protect her, or to show off for her, the dandy next would tip his hand in some way.

Half an hour later, though, they reached the outskirts of the town and nothing had happened. Payson had to hand it to the dandy. He kept cool under pressure. He had not given the slightest indication of fear.

Payson turned away from the wagon and was halfway through the town before he realized that the dandy's lack of response was a sign in itself. Any ordinary man would have been shaking in his boots. How could a dandy like him have remained so calm?

At nine o'clock that night, the coach Amy had watched leave Casper early that morning was halfway between Goose Egg and Casper on its return trip. There were no passengers this trip, only the driver and shotgun guard, the same two who had taken the run out this morning. They had been working hard for fifteen hours, and now both of them were on the edge of exhaustion.

Tomorrow another driver and guard would take the stage out, and Deekus and Billy would have one day to rest. For a while they had talked about what they would do on their day off, but even talk grew tiring, and now they were both nodding, fighting the sleep that threatened to overtake them. Deekus was driving, and because he had something to do, it was a little easier for him to stay awake than it was for Billy. That was why, when the two masked men suddenly appeared in the road in front of them, Billy did not even see them until Deekus braked the stage to an abrupt stop.

"Hold on here, Deekus, what are you tryin' to do, throw me outta my seat?" Billy asked gruffly.

"Wake up, Billy," Deekus hissed. "We've got company."

"What?" Then Billy saw the two men astride their horses, both holding double-barreled shotguns leveled toward Deekus and him. Billy started to reach for his rifle, but Deekus stuck out his hand to stop him.

"Don't be a fool, boy. They got the drop on us."

"You better listen to the old man, kid," one of the riders said. His words were muffled, because he, like his partner, was wearing a mask.

"Throw down the money," the other robber demanded.

"You ain't gettin' nothin' off this coach," Billy said.

"Do it, Billy," Deekus said.

"Damn!" Billy swore. Opening the strongbox, he picked up the money pouch and threw it down onto the ground. "Damn, damn, damn!"

"Don't take it so bad, boy," one of the riders said. "There are shotgun guards lots older'n you who gave up their loot. You'll get over it. Driver, get this team on outta here."

Deekus neither answered nor waited for a second invitation. Instead he snapped his whip over the team, and the horses leaped ahead. Billy suddenly felt a shock of recognition in what he had just witnessed, and he stood up and looked back toward the outlaws.

"Deekus, that fella in the green shirt is—"

"Hush up, boy," Deekus hissed. "You got somethin' to say, say it to the sheriff when we get back. They ain't no sense in lettin' them know you recognized them."

"Holdup! The stage was held up!" Billy shouted as they drove into town an hour later.

Deekus braked the coach to a sliding stop in front of the Crystal Palace, and Angus Hightower met them on the front porch. Billy's shout brought several others as well.

"What happened, Deekus?" Angus asked.

"There was two of 'em," Deekus said. "They took the money."

"You couldn't stop them?" Angus asked Billy.

"I tried—" Billy began.

"It weren't the boy's fault," Deekus interrupted. "And I won't have you blamin' him. They was there afore we knew it, and they had the drop on us with shotguns."

"I'm real sorry, Mr. Hightower, but there weren't nothin' I could do," Billy apologized.

"Don't worry about it," Angus said. "I'm just glad neither one of you was hurt."

"How much did they get, Angus?" the sheriff asked, pushing his way through the crowd that had arrived before him.

"I don't know. I haven't seen the shipping bill," Angus said.

"It was fourteen hundred and eleven dollars," Deekus said, handing the bill to Angus.

"There!" Billy suddenly shouted. He pointed to two men who were standing on the corner of the porch, right next to Charlie Payson. "Them was the two that held us up."

"Are you certain?" the sheriff asked.

"I'm certain all right," Billy said. "One of 'em was tall with red hair, and the other was short with black hair. Them's the two."

The sheriff looked over at the two men. Neither of them was native to Casper, but they had been quite visible around town over the last few days, usually in the company of Payson.

"You two fellas want to tell me where you were tonight?" he asked.

"They were with me, over in Glenrock," Payson said. "We were in a card game. You can check it out if you want."

"That's right, sheriff. We just got back," the tall redhead said. "We was over in the Angry Bull across the street havin' a drink just now, when we heard all the commotion."

"Can anybody else vouch for you? How about you, Mike? You're tending bar at the Angry Bull tonight, aren't you?"

"Sure am."

"Can you say where they were?"

"I can't say whether they were in Glenrock or not, but I did see all three of 'em come into our place together," Mike answered.

"All right," the sheriff said. "I'm not going to hold you fellas now, but don't go anywhere for a while."

"What do you mean?" Billy shouted. "You ain't gonna just let 'em go, are you, sheriff? They robbed the stage."

"I thought you said the robbers were wearing masks," the sheriff said.

"They was."

"Then how do you know it was these two?"

Billy looked puzzled for a moment and then said stubbornly, "I know, that's all. Tell 'em, Deekus."

Deekus looked at the two men closely. "I wish to hell I could be as certain as the boy," Deekus said. "But the truth is, it was dark; they was wearing masks and hats, and my eyes ain't as good as they once was. I think it was them, I truly do, but I couldn't swear to it in court."

"That's it, then," the sheriff said. "There's nothing I can do."

Chapter Five

It was two o'clock in the morning, but Smith lay fully awake on the bed in his room with his hands folded behind his head. A candle burned on the bedside table, and a wavering yellow-orange light washed over the walls. The flickering light had a hypnotic effect, and without intending to, Smith found himself remembering in vivid detail. . . .

Captain Butler was with a handful of riders, waiting under a cluster of trees near the town of Lawrence, Kansas. It was snowing, and he and the others wore sheepskin coats. Their hats already covered with snow, they were waiting for a Yankee ambulance to come by, because they had learned from Quantrill that the ambulance would be carrying a payroll shipment.

"Ya'll really think the Yankees will come out in weather like this?" one of the men asked. He squirted a stream of tobacco juice into a snowbank, where it stayed brown for just a moment before being covered by the falling snow.

"They'll be here," a young man said.

"What makes you think so?"

" 'Cause the major said they'd be here."

"Yeah? Well, how come you're always willin' to take as gospel ever' thing Quantrill says? He got a pocket full o' sugar titties for you or somethin'?"

The young soldier who had defended Quantrill unbuttoned his coat and faced his challenger, the movement exposing his pistol. His hand moved over it. "I'm gonna shoot you, you son of a bitch," he said. "I'm gonna gut-shoot you and watch you die slow."

Captain Butler, who was in charge of the group, moved his horse between the hotheaded boy and the man who had taunted him. "Jesse," he said, addressing the younger soldier, "we don't have enough men to be killing our own. Let it be."

"Nobody talks to Jesse James like that an' gets away with it," the youth protested.

Butler turned to Jesse's older brother. "Frank, either calm him down, or take him back to the camp," he ordered.

Frank rode over to Jesse and put his hand on his shoulder.

"Jesse, close your coat, will you? You're gonna catch your death of a chill."

There was a moment of tension, and then Jesse smiled easily. He buttoned his coat.

"Sure, Frank, if you say so," Jesse said.

"Ha, I thought you might . . ." the challenger started to say, but he never finished his statement because Butler had his own pistol out and cocked so fast it was a blur. He shoved the barrel of it into the man's face.

"What the hell? What are you doin'?" the frightened man asked.

"If you keep this up it's going to erupt into a fight," Butler said calmly. "Folks will start choosing sides. Two or three or four might be killed, and I'll be short of men. I'd be better off to just kill you now and cut my losses."

"Hold on! You don't mean that!"

"Try it and find out."

"All right, all right, I was just funnin' the boy. I didn't mean nothin' by it."

Butler moved away from the others and waited on the side of the road for the ambulance. He looked at the men with him, from the young, seventeen-year-old Jesse James to the fifty-nine-year-old Carter True. They had been at war for four long years now. Some had been farmers before the war, some had been outlaws, but their lives had not been changed as drastically as his.

At the urging of his father Butler had come home from his grand concert tour of Europe to fight in the war, and he had begun his campaign with the Fourth Mississippi, a cavalry unit. At the time, he had thought war meant flags snapping in the wind, gallant charges across fields of battle, clashing sabers, and spirited horses. But when his commander learned that the fingers that caressed the piano keys with such skill could be equally skillful with a pistol and rifle, Butler was selected to be a sharpshooter. Not long after, during the battle of Shiloh, he was strategically placed in a commanding position behind a rock and told to kill Yankees.

Butler killed enemy soldiers, not amid the clash and clang of sabers, but with the silent whisper of a bullet, fired from three hundred yards away. Men dressed in blue who had no idea they were in danger, who never suspected their killer was drawing a bead on them, fell before his deadly accurate shooting. For three days Butler slaughtered them, shooting until his rifle barrel became so hot that he had to use rags to hold it. He killed without seeing their faces, and he killed until he lost count of the bodies. He killed until he was sick of killing.

There were thirty thousand men in gray and blue killed or wounded during that battle. Butler's own father, a colonel on General Albert Sidney Johnston's staff, was one of those killed, felled by the same bursting cannon ball that killed his commander. For three days the wounded of both sides lay in the glaring sun by day and in driving thunderstorms by night. Where there had been two armies on the field, there were now three: the blue, the gray, and the bloodied. Enemies when they came to the field, they were now united in pain and death; and in the early morning hours, after the storms had subsided, their pitiful cries drowned out the thrum of frogs and trill of insects. When it was all over, nothing had been accomplished.

Butler wanted no more of war on such an impersonal basis. He would continue to fight for the South, for that was what he was sworn to do, but he would no longer kill men from the isolation of cover and distance. He left the organized cavalry and joined Quantrill, thinking that smaller, guerrilla operations would make the war more personal and, somehow, more honorable.

But that was not the way it was. Quantrill had attracted men like Jesse and Frank James; Jim, Bob, and Cole Younger; and dozens of others of the same ilk. They were totally unconcerned with how their activities tied in with the rest of the war; they did not, in fact, even care how the war came out. Theirs was a personal war, often fought for personal gain, and Butler became a part of it because there was nothing else left for him.

Through the muffling shroud of the snowfall, Captain Butler heard the whistle and shout of the ambulance driver urging his team on.

"All right," he said to the others. "I hear them coming."

"How far away?"

"Not too far. I'm going to ride out and stop them."

"How you gonna do that?"

"They're in an ambulance, aren't they? I'm going to tell them I have an injured man."

"Yeah, but it ain't really an ambulance."

"We aren't supposed to know that. My hope is he will stop, at least long enough to yell at me to get out of the road. When he does that, we can hit them. If we're lucky, we'll be able to take the payroll without firing a shot."

Butler positioned the rest of the men back in the trees, and then he rode out into the road and waited.

The ruse worked. The ambulance driver stopped the ambulance, and three men stepped out of the wagon, holding their rifles at the ready.

"What is it?" the driver asked. "What do you want?"

"I've got a wounded man, I need—" That was as far as Butler got. A volley of shots rang out from the treeline, and the three soldiers and driver fell dead.

Butler looked on in surprise and shock, and then he twisted around in his saddle.

"Who told you to fire?" he shouted angrily.

"What difference does it make, Captain, whether we

kill them now or later?" one of his men asked. "You know the major won't keep no prisoners."

The man was speaking of Quantrill, and Butler knew that he was right. So much, he thought, for a more personal war being more honorable. . . .

Smith swung his legs over the side of his bed and sat up. He pinched the bridge of his nose as if to force the unpleasant memories away.

Walking over to the window, he breathed in the fresh air. Although it was after two in the morning, he could still hear laughter from the Angry Bull. The saloon offered none of the amenities of the Crystal Palace, but stayed in business because its doors did not close until the morning light began to spill through its streaked windows. Out on the prairie a coyote howled, and in town a dog, responding to some primordial urge, answered the call. Smith stood in the window for a long moment and then turned back, snuffed out the candle, and went to bed.

It took only three days for the new Coaltree Cross-country Express Company depot to be framed up. The day the roof went on, even before the carpenters and painters were finished, Wes DuMont moved in. He had picked up a letter from the post office this morning—ironically, delivered by Wyoming Rapid Express, which had the mail contract—and now he sat at his new desk to read it:

Per your instructions, three additional coaches have been sent by train to Medicine Bow. However, we are unable to provide you with an operating budget, as there have been no specific instructions from Mr. Percy Rawlings of the home office to do so.

As Mr. Coaltree is expected in Casper, perhaps you could have him authorize the operating funds. Until such time as we have received written orders, either from Percy Rawlings or from Mr. Coaltree himself, no money can be made available for this purpose.

Angrily, DuMont wadded up the letter. He had no intention of contacting San Francisco for authorization. In the first place, he was not at all sure they would approve the operation. And even if they did, it would dilute what he was trying to do. His goal was to meet Ben Coaltree when he arrived and not only present his daughter to him, but also deliver a new stage route.

Such initiative, he was sure, would be well received by Ben Coaltree. In addition DuMont believed he now enjoyed a certain position of favor with Coaltree's daughter. His future looked bright indeed.

But his road to success was not proving to be an entirely smooth one. He had already hired several men, and the expenses were mounting. He would have to meet his first payroll in a week. If he failed to meet it, it could just be that his carefully laid scheme would collapse. How ironic it would be, he thought, if Angus Hightower won out because DuMont was short of money. That was a secret that he had to guard with his life. As far as everyone else was concerned, he must appear to have more than enough money to carry out his plan.

DuMont thought about what he had to do. If he could break Hightower quickly enough, before anyone got wind of how dangerously low on money he really was, then everything would be all right. He had enough money to last for a little while. He had been advanced two thousand dollars in cash to be used for Amy's living expenses, and so far he had not needed to spend a cent of it. Her very name had been enough for the hotel to extend credit. That would allow him to use the cash. That was not the purpose intended for the money, but he was sure that Ben Coaltree would understand. After all, Coaltree was not only a businessman, he was man who appreciated risks.

Nevertheless, he would have to think of something to speed things up. The longer it took, the stronger Angus Hightower's position would be.

"Mr. DuMont?"

DuMont looked up to see Blair Morann, the man he had hired to run the Casper station.

"Yes, Morann, what is it?" DuMont stuck the wadded-up letter into his pocket.

"I've got the sign painter out here. He wants to know if you want the name on the window, or a big sign to go on top of the building. The big sign would cost more."

"I want both," DuMont said.

"Both?"

"Yes, both. Morann, the people of Casper have got to know that Coaltree is no penny-pinching operation. We've got to make a splash, man, a big splash."

Morann smiled. "Yes, sir. I'll tell him both."

"Good, good. And how about the waiting benches. Are they ready yet?"

"The carpenter's working on them."

"Stay on it, Morann."

"Yes, sir," Morann said. "Let me tell you, Mr. DuMont, it's awful good to be workin' again, and especially for an outfit like Coaltree."

Morann, DuMont knew, had once worked for Angus Hightower. Hightower had fired him when a money shipment turned up a little short. Morann had denied having anything to do with the missing money, accusing Angus of unscrupulous business practices.

From everything DuMont had been able to learn, Morann actually had stolen the hundred dollars, but he pretended to believe Morann's side of the story. Morann was experienced, and he had a grudge against Angus. That was the kind of man DuMont wanted until Hightower was run out of business. After that happened, DuMont would fire Morann, and then—he was proud of this little stroke of genius—he would hire Angus Hightower himself to run the operation in Casper, thereby capitalizing on the goodwill Angus had already established in the community.

In the midst of all his self-congratulation, however, DuMont thought again of the need to speed things up. He had to have control of Wyoming Rapid Express within three weeks, or he was going to lose everything. It was time to take a few steps.

Smith had been playing requests all evening. The song most requested was "Buffalo Gals," but occasionally someone would get a bit nostalgic and request "Lorene" or "Just Before the Battle, Mother." He was on one of the merrier numbers when Billy Sinclair came in.

Billy, who after a day off was just beginning to enjoy his free time, was wearing his fast-draw gun rig low on his hips. He stood at the bar, telling of his trick-shooting exploits, giving demonstrations of gun twirling and generally having a good time as he provided free entertainment.

Two of the women who worked at the Crystal Palace were with him, and though Billy was pleased by their attention, he kept glancing toward Amy, to see if she was noticing him. He knew she was older, but so were the other women. And though he did not harbor any real intentions toward her, it pleased him to flirt with her, even in such an indirect way.

"I've got a new trick," Billy was saying in a voice loud enough for everyone to hear. "What I do is, I put a silver dollar on the back of my hand, then hold my hand out in front of me. I turn my hand and the silver dollar slides off. Then, I draw my pistol and shoot, hitting the silver dollar before it hits the ground."

"Can you really do that, Billy?" one of the women asked.

"You better believe I can," Billy answered, beaming proudly.

Wes DuMont came into the saloon and saw Billy holding court.

"Hey, Mr. DuMont. You're going to be around on the Fourth of July, aren't you?" Billy called.

"I certainly intend to be."

"Then you sure don't want to miss my trick-shooting exhibition. It'll be the best you ever saw."

"One thing about Billy," someone said. "He ain't the shy, modest type."

Everyone laughed.

DuMont saw Amy and invited her over to his table. "Won't you take supper with me?" he asked.

Amy really did not want to, but she had no legitimate reason to turn him down, so she accepted his invitation.

"Did you see the stages arrive this afternoon?" DuMont asked. "We beat Hightower's stage by half an hour. That's what will get customers to come over to us. Hard work and efficient operation."

"I'm afraid I didn't notice," Amy said.

"You should pay attention to these things, Amy. After all, it is your father's business, and you—"

"Wes . . ." Amy said, interrupting him with a frightened voice. She put her hand on his arm.

"What is it? You look as if you've seen a ghost."

"It's him," she said. "The one who killed the man at the way station."

DuMont turned toward the door and saw Fast Charlie Payson standing there. His entry made a dramatic impact on everyone present. Billy's bantering stopped, the laughter stilled, and conversations quieted. Now the only audible sound was the measured ticktock of the large grandfather clock that stood to one side of the room.

"You," the albino said, motioning with his gunhand in the direction of Billy Sinclair.

Billy turned away from Payson and picked up his beer. Amy could see Billy's hands trembling as he took a drink.

"I'm talkin' to you, shotgun guard. You lied about two of my friends. You tried to get them into trouble."

"I didn't lie," Billy said. "I just told the sheriff I saw two men, one tall with red hair, another short with dark hair, the same two men I saw with you the day before."

"They were in Glenrock with me," Payson said.

Billy forced himself to take another sip of his beer, trying to show a studied indifference. "That's what you told the sheriff."

"You sayin' I'm lyin'?" Payson challenged.

Now the shaking of Billy's hands was more obvious than before, and visible to everyone. He realized that Payson was serious about trying to goad him into a fight. "I'm not sayin' that," he replied.

"Well, one of us is lyin'," Payson said. "And if it ain't me, why, it must be you."

Billy did not answer.

"Say it."

"Say what?"

"Say you're lyin' through your teeth. Admit it to me and to everyone in this room."

"What?" Billy asked in a small voice.

Payson's features may have been arranged in a smile just then, though if so, it was a smile only the devil could have recognized. His mouth was stretched thin, and his hard pink eyes were narrowed. He was obviously enjoying Billy's discomfort.

"Say it. Say, 'Mr. Payson, I was lyin' through my teeth.'"

"I . . . I can't say that," Billy replied. "I told the sheriff what I saw, that's all."

"Then I guess you better use your gun."

"Oh, Wes," Amy gasped. "Do something. Stop them."

Standing, DuMont said to Payson, "I'm sure this young man didn't mean anything against you, Mr. Payson."

Payson turned his cold eyes toward DuMont. "You plannin' on buyin' into this?"

"No . . . no, of course not," DuMont said quickly. He sat back down and pulled out a handkerchief to wipe his face.

"Pull your gun," Payson ordered Billy.

"Mr. Payson, I don't want to fight you."

"Pull it."

From his seat at the piano across the room, Smith spoke calmly, "Billy, take off your gun."

"You butt out, piano player," Payson warned.

"Take off your gun, Billy," Smith spoke again in a firm voice. "Take it off, and apologize to him."

When Billy looked over at him, Smith saw that his eyes were mad with fear, like the eyes of an animal trapped in a forest fire. But behind the fear there was something else, something Smith had seen in soldiers during the war. There was the acceptance of death.

"No," Billy answered. His chin was trembling and there was a line of perspiration on his upper lip. "It'd be all right for you, but I couldn't live with myself."

"Billy, no," Smith said quietly, making it almost a plea.

Billy turned to face Payson. There were awkward hasty sounds, then, of tables and chairs scraping on the floor as everyone began moving out of the way. Billy wiped the palm of his hand on his pants leg.

"Go for it any time you're ready, boy," Payson challenged, in a voice that sounded for all the world like the threatening hiss of a serpent.

Billy went for his pistol. He was fast, nearly as fast as the albino, and had he been a little older and wiser, had he known that he had to kill, he might have stood a chance. As it was, Payson fired while Billy was still thinking about it, and Billy caught the bullet in his lungs. His eyes opened wide, as if in surprise, and he then hit the edge of the bar and slid down to the floor in a sitting position. His chest was sucking air, and he weakly coughed blood.

Smith hurried over to him.

"I . . . I'm dying, aren't I, Smith?" Billy asked. There was as much curiosity as fear in the question.

"Yes," Smith said.

"I . . . I didn't know it would be like this," Billy gasped. His head fell back against the bar, but his eyes remained open, and Smith watched the light in them fade as the boy died.

"He's dead," Smith said.

"Everyone saw it," Payson declared. "It was a fair fight."

There were footfalls on the wooden porch, and half a dozen people ran inside to see what happened. One of them was the sheriff, who immediately saw Billy, still sitting upright, his chest covered with blood, his hand down by his side, and his unfired gun on the floor beside him.

"What happened here?" he asked.

"Ask them," Payson said. He poured himself a drink.

Reluctantly, all the witnesses agreed that, though Billy had been sorely provoked, it had been a fair fight.

"Is this all there is to it?" Amy asked the lawman, when he had finished questioning the witnesses.

"What would you have me do, miss?" the sheriff asked.

"Put him in jail."

"I can't put a man in jail for defending himself."

"Defending himself? Didn't you hear what everyone said? He provoked Billy into fighting him."

"Yes'm, but I also heard witnesses say that the piano player told Billy to take off his pistol and apologize. Now, if the boy had done that, there wouldn't have been a fight. I'm sorry, but there's nothing I can do." The sheriff looked over at Payson.

"Mr. Payson, are you going to be staying in town much longer?"

"I've got some business to tend to," Payson said.

"You got any idea how much longer that business is going to take?"

Payson tossed his drink down and glared at the sheriff.

"It'll take as long as it takes," he said.

When Angus learned about the killing later that evening, he was enraged that Payson was going to get away with it. He wanted to go across the street to the Angry Bull, stand up to Payson, and call him a killer to his face. Marybeth, Amy, Smith, and even Wes DuMont hastened to talk him out of it.

"Don't be a fool, Hightower," DuMont said. "You wouldn't stand a chance against someone like him. I want to run you out of business, but I don't want to see you killed."

"Don't make the same mistake Billy made," Smith said. "Billy was afraid."

"Afraid? But Billy went against him," Angus said.

"Yes," Smith replied. "He stood up to him because he was afraid not to. You have more courage than that."

"Listen to them, Angus. They're making sense," Marybeth said.

"I guess you're right," Angus finally agreed. "It's just that I hate to see him get away with it."

"One day Payson will brace the wrong man," Smith said. "When he does, he's going down."

DuMont gave a short, derisive laugh. "What do you know about things like that? Stick to your music, piano player. You'll live longer."

Smith looked at DuMont, his eyes flashing a steely cold hostility. The look unnerved DuMont, though he did not know why. He hastily turned away from Smith to talk to Angus.

"I guess Billy's getting killed is going to cause you a problem, isn't it, Hightower? You've got a money shipment to make tomorrow, and no one to guard it. If you would like, you can ship it on our stage at no extra cost. As I said, I want to run you out of business, but I don't want to take unfair advantage of your misfortunes."

"I appreciate the offer, DuMont, but I'll carry the shipment. I'll guard it myself."

"Then I'll be on that stage with you, Angus," Marybeth said. "I have some things I want to take care of in Medicine Bow."

"It would probably be safer to ride on one of our coaches," DuMont pointed out. He smiled. "Since you're a friend of Miss Coaltree's, I would be pleased to provide a complimentary ticket for you."

"Thank you, but I'm sure I would be more comfortable with Wyoming Rapid Express," Marybeth said pointedly.

"In that case, Mr. Hightower," DuMont said, "at least let me loan you a shotgun guard. I would feel better knowing that the stage is well protected."

"That won't be necessary, DuMont. I may not be fast with a pistol, but I'm damn good with a rifle. If anyone tries to get this money or bother my passengers, I'll shoot him before he gets within a hundred yards of the stage."

Chapter Six

For some time after Billy was killed, there was a buzz of excitement in the Crystal Palace. Those who had witnessed the fight shared their recall of it with those who had not been there, and the story was told and retold far into the night. Billy's last words were repeated and enhanced until they were no longer the plaintive murmurings of a dying boy, but the brave, challenging epitaph of "Quick Draw Billy."

"Am I dyin', Smith? Then I'll be waitin' for him on the other side," one version went.

The inevitable comparisons with other gunfights were drawn, and once again Rufus Butler's name was brought up. People wondered what had happened to him and how he would fare against Fast Charlie Payson.

Amy did not stay around to listen to the talk. Seeing the body at the way station had been bad enough, but witnessing an actual shooting was much worse. She was too upset to stay downstairs for dinner, so Marybeth took her upstairs, to her own apartment.

"It's like a . . . a circus or something, down there," Amy said. "The way they are talking, well, it's as if they're glorifying the event."

"Here," Marybeth spoke as she poured a brandy for the younger woman. "This might help some."

"Thank you." Amy accepted the proffered drink. The brandy was strong but good.

"Are you going to be all right?" the red-haired woman asked.

"Yes. Oh, Marybeth, is this what the West is like? I've been here less than two weeks now, and already I've seen two killings."

"And both of them by the same man." Marybeth maternally brushed back Amy's dark hair with her hand as she spoke. "No, honey, it's not always like this. I've been out here for four years, and this was the first killing that ever happened in the Crystal Palace. I won't lie to you; there have been a few fatal shootings in town, most of them across the street in the Angry Bull. But for the most part, Casper is a good, decent place to live."

"Billy was so young," Amy said. "Too young to die."

"Honey, you were in Boston during the war, weren't you?"

"Yes."

"Then let me tell you, there is no such thing as being too young to die. I saw them die on our plantation . . . young men, boys really, from both sides. Many of them lie buried in our family cemetery." There was a distant look in Marybeth's eyes for a long moment. After a pause she added, "And not all were men . . . some of them were women, some of them mothers, in the prime of life."

Amy looked at her first with surprise, and then her eyes brimmed with tears. She put her hand out to touch Marybeth. "Oh, Marybeth, I'm so sorry."

Marybeth smiled. "It was a long time ago. And they say that time heals all pain."

"Has it?"

Marybeth's eyes then filled with tears, but her smile did not fade. "Well, let's say it has at least made the pain bearable."

"I . . . I feel foolish," Amy said. "Here you are, comforting me as if I'm a baby, when you have been through so much more."

"Maybe we're comforting each other," Marybeth suggested. "Listen, I've got to get back downstairs. If you'd

like, you may stay here. You might find my apartment
more comfortable than your room."

"Thank you. I will stay a while, if you don't mind."

Marybeth kissed Amy on the forehead and then left.
Amy leaned her head back and tried to will the terrible
images from her mind. Every time she closed her eyes,
though, she could see the look of fear on Billy's face, just
before the fight, and then the blood.

She opened her eyes and looked around Marybeth's
apartment. She was in a sitting room. To her left was a
bedroom, the corner of the brass bedstead just visible
through the open door.

The sitting room had a comfortable, homey look about
it. The wallpaper was a cream color, with a blue print
design of flower-filled baskets. In addition to the settee on
which she was resting, there was a rocking chair, an
overstuffed chair, and a library table flanked by two straight-
backed chairs. Against the wall nearest the door was a
bookcase enclosed by curved glass, its shelves filled with
books.

Amy walked over to look at the books, and finding one
by Charles Dickens, pulled it out. When she opened the
cover she was surprised to see that it was inscribed:

> To Mrs. Marybeth Staley;
>
> Madam, in the wilderness I found a flower,
> In the darkness I saw a light,
> In a sea of silence, I heard a song.
> Thank you, gracious lady.
>
> Charles Dickens

What a small world, Amy thought. While in London the
year before, she had met Charles Dickens when he gave a
dramatic reading to raise money for an organization that
helped poor people relocate to Australia. As it turned out,
Dickens had less than one more month to live before he
suffered a fatal stroke.

Amy knew that Dickens had visited America three times,

and visited the West twice, once in 1867 and again in 1868. Judging from the inscription, he had stayed here, in this hotel, possibly even in the room where she was staying now.

As Amy put the book back on the shelf, she saw a photograph standing on top of the case. A handsome man in the uniform of a Confederate colonel was seated in a chair, and at his side, with her hand resting on his shoulder, was a beautiful woman. Two young boys, one blond, one dark, stood in front, holding their hats in their hands and staring seriously into the camera. Amy did not recognize the man or the boys, but the woman in the picture was Marybeth Staley.

Downstairs in the saloon, a few patrons were complaining that there was no music, so Marybeth went up to check on Smith. She saw his door open and walked down the hall to speak to him. When she looked in through the door, she saw him sitting in a chair, half a bottle of whiskey on the table beside him. The glass beside the bottle was empty. He was holding a silver-plated pistol.

"Rufus, no, please!" Marybeth said. Then, realizing she had spoken his name, she looked around quickly to make certain no one had overheard, and then she stepped into the room and closed the door.

Smith poured himself a glass of whiskey, and from the unsteady way he raised it to his lips, it was obvious this was not the first drink he had taken tonight. He held the glass up, and the liquor caught a light from the lantern and glowed as if it had captured part of the flame.

"I let him die," Smith said finally. "I let Billy Sinclair get shot down, and I did nothing to stop it."

"What could you do? You tried to talk him out of it."

"I should have stepped in and goaded the albino into drawing on me."

"You couldn't have. You didn't have a gun. And even if someone gave you one, you saw how fast he was."

Smith drained his glass and then set it rather noisily and

unsteadily on the table. "But I . . ." He spun the cylinder of his pistol and it caught a beam of light and sent slivers of silver flashing through the room. "I, my dear Aunt Marybeth, am Rufus Butler." He twisted his mouth in bitterness, and the name came out as a slur.

"And is that who you want to be?" Marybeth asked. "Do you want to be the man who is known and feared . . . and sought out by killers in every town in the West? Did you like that life when you were living it?"

"No," Smith said, painfully. "You know I didn't. But I just sat there and watched Billy be killed!"

"Rufus, you couldn't have won, no matter what happened. If you had beaten him, everyone would have known that the man they thought was Smith was actually Rufus Butler. You would have no choice but to live that life again. And if you had lost, it wouldn't have helped Billy. He would have been the next victim, and you know it."

"I . . . I suppose there is some sense to what you're saying," Smith agreed. He walked over to a trunk at the foot of his bed, lifted the lid, and put the pistol inside.

"Thank you, *Smith*," Marybeth said, emphasizing the name as she smiled at him. "Don't forget, you're my only sister's only child. You're all that's left of my family, now. I don't want anything to happen to you."

Smith gave his aunt a hug. "I won't forget," he promised. "I'll let it lie . . . for now."

Billy Sinclair had been somewhat of a show-off, but nobody had resented it. He'd been a friendly person who had known almost everyone in town by name, who had waved hello at them from his shotgun seat on the stagecoach. When he put on his trick-shooting shows, he was always kind to the older folks and always paid special attention to the children. As a result of his popularity, and because a funeral was a social event as much as a wedding or a spring dance, his funeral attracted the largest crowd to gather in Casper since the ceremonies in 1867, when the U.S. Army post had moved east to Fort Fetterman.

Billy's coffin was a tribute to him. It was finished with a shimmering black lacquer, fancied up with silver hinges and scrollwork, and lined with white satin. On the morning of the funeral his body was laid out at the Nunlee Funeral Parlor. For the viewing he was dressed in a suit and tie, though no one had ever seen him wear such clothes in life. His arms were folded across his chest, and the pistol he had been so proud of was clutched in his right hand.

The crowd followed the glass-sided hearse from the funeral home to the cemetery, where Parson Jerome MacAlister performed the graveside services. MacAlister had been preaching in Casper for over five years, and he had never before had such a crowd in his church. Bristling with pride, he preached what he was sure was the best sermon he had ever given. Pleased by the number of wet eyes he saw, he was convinced that the people had been moved by his words, forgetting that the tears expressed sorrow over the death of a popular young man.

Smith had driven Marybeth and Amy to the funeral. As they were leaving the cemetery after the interment, DuMont walked over toward them. He was holding his hat in his hand.

"It's a sad day," he said.

"Yes," Amy answered.

"I wish the boy had listened to you, Smith. If he had, he'd still be alive."

"Maybe," Smith said. "But from the way Payson pushed the fight, I think he intended to kill Billy no matter what."

"Maybe now that he has killed again, he'll move on to some other place," DuMont suggested. "Except I don't suppose it works that way."

"I don't suppose it does," Smith said.

"Oh, Miss Staley," DuMont said, "are you still determined to take the Wyoming Rapid Express stage to Medicine Bow, tomorrow?"

"Yes. Why?"

"No particular reason, I guess. It's just that, what with the robbery of the Rapid Express coach the other day and

the killing of Billy yesterday, riding on one of Mr. Hightower's coaches might not be the safest thing to do."

"Is that your tactic now, DuMont?" Smith asked. "Are
you saying it's dangerous to ride on any stage but yours?"

"Actually, no, I was merely expressing some concern for
Miss Staley's safety," DuMont replied. "But, in fact, there
is something to be said for such a claim. After all, none of
my stages have been robbed, none of my employees killed."

"Thank you for your concern," Marybeth said. "But I'll
be riding with Angus."

"I'm sure there will be no trouble," DuMont said. He
nodded at them. "Ladies," he said, as he excused himself.

"I don't like that man," Marybeth exclaimed as DuMont
walked away.

When the stage left at six o'clock the next morning,
Deekus was at the reins and Angus was handling shotgun
duties. Marybeth was the lone passenger.

The main street was quiet and gray with early morning
light. The boardwalks were empty, and even the dog that
chased the stage out of town did so without barking, as if
aware of the earliness of the hour.

The trip to Medicine Bow was made without incident,
and the money shipment Angus had to deliver was turned
over to the bank. Marybeth attended to her business in
short order and was ready to go when the stage was due to
leave for its return trip to Casper. As she had been that
morning, she was again the only passenger.

"Deekus, we aren't carrying anything of particular value,"
Angus said, as they got ready to leave, "so if you don't
mind, I'm going to ride down in the coach with Miss
Staley."

"Don't mind at all, boss," Deekus said. "You go right
ahead."

Angus got into the coach and laid his rifle on the floor.
He tossed his hat on the seat beside him and smiled at
Marybeth, who was sitting across from him.

"You don't mind the company, do you?"

"Of course not, but I'm sorry to see it like this."

"What do you mean?"

"It looks as though I'm your only paying passenger," Marybeth explained. "You can't make any money this way."

"Well, the coach can't be full every time," Angus told her. "And if we are going to be a scheduled stage line, we have to maintain a schedule, even if only one person, or nobody, rides."

"I know it isn't nice of me, but I hope the Coaltree stage is empty."

Angus chuckled. "I checked at the depot," he said. "The only passengers they've carried for the last three days have been their own employees."

"Good."

Above them, they heard Deekus whistle to the team and then the explosive pop of his whip. The horses strained into their harness, and the coach lurched forward to begin its long journey home.

Marybeth and Angus talked of easy, familiar things for the first two hours of the journey. At their first stop, the Freeland way station, they got out for a while and stretched their legs, then climbed back in for the next part of the trip. It was then that Marybeth took a deep breath and began the conversation she had been rehearsing in her mind.

"Angus Hightower, I think the time has come for me to tell you all about myself," she said.

"Marybeth, you don't have to—" Angus started, but Marybeth held out her hand to silence him.

"I know I don't have to. I know the way of folks out here is to tell as little as possible about who they are and where they came from. But I come from a place where a person's background is important." She smiled. "When I was a young woman, every time I met a young man at church, or at a social, my father would always ask the same question: 'Who are his people?' He believed that no relationship could get serious until that vital bit of information was exchanged."

Angus nodded quietly.

"I guess what I'm getting at, Angus Hightower, is this. Am I presuming too much if I tell you about myself? I should ask if you would like to hear."

"Of course I would like to hear."

Marybeth brushed her hand through her hair. "I don't want to tell you all this just to satisfy your curiosity. Please understand, I want to tell you because when a relationship begins to get serious, I, like my father, feel that vital information should be exchanged. Now, I ask you, is our relationship serious enough for this?"

Angus looked at Marybeth for a long time, and for a few heart-stopping moments she feared she had gone too far, pushed too hard, perhaps disrupting the delicate balance they had constructed between them.

But at last Angus spoke. "Yes, Marybeth Staley," he said. "I believe it is."

Marybeth let out a sigh and then smiled. "Oh, my," she said. She brushed her hair back and said again, "Oh, my."

Angus reached across the gap between the seats and took her hand. He held it in one of his own and patted it gently with his other hand. "Tell me, Marybeth, who *are* your people?" he asked quietly.

"My father was Harlan Prescott, the son of Casper Prescott of Warwick, Virginia," she said. "My father attended the College of William and Mary in Williamsburg, Virgina, then relocated to Smith County, Mississippi. There he bought four thousand acres of wooded land, cleared enough acres for planting, and turned it into one of the best farms in Mississippi. He married my mother, Melinda Hughes of Hinds County, when he was twenty-eight. I had a sister who was ten years older than I was, and a brother who was five years younger. I was raised in luxury, surrounded by beautiful things and by people who loved me."

Marybeth had started the discourse almost as if giving a prepared talk, and indeed she had practiced it in her mind. But the lilt of her voice faltered occasionally as she went on.

"My sister, Sarah, was the first of us children to be married. She was a heroine to me. I looked up to her in every respect . . . even physically, since she was a tall woman, and slender and strong. At any rate, within a year after her marriage she had a son, and I adored him. I held him in my arms and dandled him on my knee. I knew my sister had a penchant for poetry and the arts, but still I was amazed that by the time he was six years old, Sarah's son was giving informal piano recitals at Rose Hall, their plantation. I just would not ever have believed such a thing was possible, but I was there to see it. This little sprout of a boy could play the piano just like a duckling can swim. . . ." Marybeth's voice trailed off.

"But then my sister fell ill with a sudden brutal fever, and she died even before the doctors could make a diagnosis. It was the first tragedy in our family, and from that time on, Sarah's son became like my own." Marybeth stopped talking again for a moment and took a deep breath before resuming.

"I was married when I was seventeen," she continued. "My husband was Tom Staley. Tom was quite a bit older than I was . . . but he was a wonderful man, from good people." She looked up at Angus and smiled. "Tom's first wife had died giving birth, and their child had died two days later. It took poor Tom a long time to get over it. He didn't want any children when we first got married . . . he was frightened by what had happened to Amanda, his first wife, and he argued that my sister's boy was near enough, living at Rose Hall with his father, and close enough in temperament and blood ties to be looked upon as our son. But I insisted, and before long Tom and I had two sons of our very own, Matt and Mark.

"Trailback—that was the name of our plantation—was alive with the sound of the boys at play, fighting, running, doing everything that boys do when they are boys. Matt and Mark just worshiped their older cousin, who came often to stay with us, and our boys visited him just as often at Rose Hall. They were always active, always on the run together; the only time they were ever still for more than two minutes was when he would play the piano for them."

"Play the piano?" Angus said. He drew in a sharp breath. "Marybeth, look here, are you telling me that Smith—"

"Is my nephew, yes," Marybeth finished. Her hand slipped from his, and she shifted her position on the seat.

Angus sat back and smiled. "I've always wondered about you two. Your accents are just alike, and I felt certain you knew each other before you came here."

"Why didn't you ask?"

"I didn't figure it was any of my business."

"Don't you understand? I want it to be your business."

"I know now," Angus said. "And I'm glad you feel that way. Please, go on with your story."

Marybeth looked out the window. The sun was nearly down, a red disk just touching the western horizon. Shadows were already darkening the notches and ravines in the hills.

Marybeth was quiet for a long moment, and Angus knew that the story was becoming more difficult for her to share.

"When the war came," Marybeth went on, "my husband formed a group of volunteer cavalry. He, my father, and my brother-in-law, who was Smith's father, were all appointed colonels in the Army of the Confederacy, ready to turn back the despot's heel. Oh, we had a grand party before they left."

Angus saw that tears were now streaking down her cheeks.

"Little did we realize that not one of those three men would be alive a year later. My father was the first to go. He didn't die a very glamorous death, I'm afraid. He died of dysentery, contracted while they were still in camp. My husband was killed in a little town in Missouri called New Madrid, and Smith's father was killed at Shiloh.

"Mark, my youngest son, died of a malady the doctors were unable to diagnose or treat, suspiciously similar to the sickness that killed my sister, Sarah. Matt, my oldest, following some misguided Southern sense of honor, be-

came a drummer boy. He was killed at a place called Cold
Harbor. I got a nice letter from his commanding officer."

Marybeth looked down at her hands, the tears falling
onto them, and Angus reached over and took them into
his.

"We didn't even get the name of the place where my
brother was killed," she continued. "He marched away
one fine spring morning and never came back. Within
another year my mother was dead from an outbreak of
cholera, and I was the only one left. There was no one to
work the farms, and so the fields went to weed, and the
houses at Rose Hall and my father's place were burned.
Then, after the war, all three estates were taken for back
taxes. I had no family, no money, and finally no place to
live."

Angus raised her hands to his lips and kissed them
gently. "But you had your nephew," he suggested, attempting to find a ray of sunlight amidst all the dark
clouds.

"Ah, yes, I had my nephew. How can I tell you about
Smith? Though he later came back from the war un-
scratched, he was as much a victim as those unfortunate
men who lost an arm or leg. I'm afraid he lost something
much more dear, even though it isn't visible. He lost a
part of his soul. He was a dear, gentle, sweet boy who
wanted only to give beauty to the world. Instead, he was
scarred by the world's ugliness."

"Smith isn't his real name, is it?" Angus asked.

"As a matter of fact it *is* his middle name, after the
county where he was born. He has his reasons for wanting
to use that name instead of the name he was known by.
But I . . . I'd rather not go into that just yet."

"It isn't necessary," Angus said. It was dark outside the
stage now, and the moon was a bright orb that bathed the
hills in silver. "How did you come to Casper?"

"I couldn't stay in Mississippi anymore," Marybeth said,
wiping the tears from her face. "There was nothing for me
there. When Smith came back after the War, he had some
money . . . he didn't tell me where it came from, and I

didn't ask him. He insisted that I use it to get a new start.
I took a boat upriver to St. Louis, stayed there awhile,
took a job teaching school, and thought about settling
there, but eventually I took the train west. When the train
stopped in Medicine Bow, I got off. I had to get off," she
laughed, "because that was as far as the Union Pacific
tracks went at the time."

Angus's soft laughter joined with hers for a moment.

"Well, Medicine Bow wasn't much of a town, and I
considered turning around and heading back to St. Louis,
but the name of Casper on the map caught my eye. You
know how some things just seem to be fated? You'll remember, my grandfather's name was Casper, and I thought
perhaps the name of the town was symbolic. So I came up
here to take a look. The stages coming up here were few
and far between in those days, since the railroad was now
going through Medicine Bow, and since Fort Casper had
recently been abandoned. I arrived here only to find that
the town, which just a few months earlier had been boom-
ing, was now in a real slump. It was still an attractive
place; it hadn't started to deteriorate yet, and I had it in
mind to start a boardinghouse, since the town was on the
route from the new Fort Fetterman down to Medicine
Bow. Then I found out that the Casper Hotel was for sale
at a reasonable price, and the Crystal Palace was part of
the deal." She laughed with pleasure, her memories of the
tragedies she had recounted now once again in the past.

"I never dreamed I would wind up a tavern keeper,"
Marybeth continued, "but then, I never dreamed I'd do
anything but live out my life in protected seclusion at
Trailback. So I figured as long as I was starting a new life
anyway, I might as well start it as far from the old as I
possibly could. But even so, the Crystal Palace was a
symbol for me. It was much like the Old South. It was
somewhat out of place and out of time. The bottom had
dropped out of Casper's future, it seemed, and the owners
of the Crystal Palace were almost willing to give it away. I
bought the whole place for a song, from the two military
men who built it, and here I am. Within a few months the

mass exodus from Casper had stopped, and the community began to revive. Not long afterward my dear nephew, Smith, came here to stay with me, and now it's my home. I don't know what my father or my husband would say if they could see me today."

"They would tell you how proud they are of you for getting on with your life."

Marybeth let out a long sigh and then said, "Now, Angus Hightower. What about you? Who are your people?"

"Yes. Well, I—"

Whatever Angus was about to say was interrupted by the sound of a gunshot. Surprised, he looked through the window into the deepening dusk in time to see a gun flash and to hear another shot.

"Mr. Hightower, there's a couple of riders chasin' us!" Deekus shouted down. He whistled at the horses, and the team broke into a gallop.

The two riders fired again. They were shooting pistols from galloping horses, fifty yards away in the dark. Because of their distance, Angus did not consider them much of an immediate threat. Still, it was not safe to be on the receiving end of gunfire, even incompetent gunfire. There was always the very real chance of a stray bullet.

Angus grabbed his rifle from the floor and leaned out the window to fire at the two riders, using the flame patterns of their shooting as his target. As his rifle barked, the muzzle flash lit up the inside of the coach for just an instant, like the brilliant, brief illumination of a flash of lightning.

"Angus, what are they after?" Marybeth asked. "You said we aren't carrying any money."

"I don't know what they want," Angus admitted. He fired, jacked in another shell, and fired again. From the top of the stage he could hear Deekus firing his pistol as well.

The two riders chased the stage for some time, but they never gained. Angus was beginning to believe that they did not actually intend to catch up to them. He found himself wondering if the attack was designed just to frighten the occupants of the coach. After all, if the riders had wanted to, it would have been an easy matter for them to stop the stage on an upgrade.

Finally the ambushers disappeared into the night, dropping back on the trail, and Deekus was able to slow the exhausted team. After a few minutes of walking the horses to cool them down, he stopped them to give them a rest, and Angus and Marybeth got out of the stage.

"Do you think they're still around?" Marybeth asked anxiously.

"No, I believe they're gone," Angus said, holding his rifle. "But just to be safe, I'd better ride up with Deekus the rest of the way." Angus used the wheel to climb up to the driver's box. He reloaded his rifle while Deekus stood on the top of the stage to look around. "See anything?" Angus asked.

"Nope. Not a thing."

"Marybeth, you better get back in. Come on, Deekus. Let's get into town."

It was after eleven when they finally pulled into Casper. Angus had Deekus stop in front of the sheriff's office, and the three of them went inside.

The deputy was sitting at the desk, drinking a cup of coffee and looking at the pictures in the latest issue of *Harper's Weekly*. There was one loudly snoring man in the jail cell, apparently a drunk sleeping it off.

"Where's the sheriff?" Angus asked the deputy.

"Over to the Angry Bull."

"Get him," Angus ordered.

The deputy walked over to the door, shouted to someone across the street to get the sheriff, and then came back inside. He got some cups and poured all three of them coffee. They were drinking it, gratefully, when the sheriff came in a moment later.

"My God, Angus, what is it? You weren't robbed again, were you?"

"No," Angus answered. "But it wasn't because they didn't try. We had two men jump us tonight, sheriff."

"Did you get a good look at them?"

"No. It was dark and they were too far away," Angus said. "But I know who they were. They were those two friends of Payson's."

The sheriff sighed and stroked his chin. "Angus, come on. If you didn't get a look at them, how can you say that?"

"Who else could it be?" Angus asked. "Sheriff, I don't care what that albino gunslinger said. I believed Billy."

"Me, too," Deekus said.

"Hell, Deekus, you were with Billy the first time," the sheriff said. "You were right there, but you said yourself you couldn't be sure."

"I said I wasn't as sure as Billy," Deekus defended. "But I also told you that I believed it was Payson's two friends. Just like I believe it was them that hit us tonight."

"The same two?"

"The same two," Deekus said.

"How close did they get to you?"

"No closer than fifty yards," Angus said.

The sheriff shook his head. "Angus, do you think a court would accept your identification of them? By your own admission they didn't get any closer than fifty yards, and it was pitch black. When Deekus saw them in the middle of the day, he couldn't identify them. Besides, they had an alibi the other day, and I have no doubt but they'll have one for tonight."

"I have no doubt either," Angus said with a sigh, "about their having an alibi and about the fact that they were the ones who did it."

"But you do see my problem, don't you?"

"Yes," Angus agreed grimly.

The sheriff put his hand on Angus's shoulder. "Believe me, Angus, I want whoever is doing this as much as you do. But I can't arrest them on someone's feelings. I've got to have something real, something that'll convince a judge and jury to hold them. When you give me that, I'll throw them in jail, that's a promise."

"All right, sheriff. If that's the way it is," Angus said.

He looked over at Marybeth. "Come on, Marybeth. I'll walk you home."

Marybeth took his arm as they stepped out of the sheriff's office. She was aware that although she had told Angus everything about her own past, he had shared nothing with her. She was not sure when they would get another opportunity like the one they had tonight, but it did not matter. She had told Angus, in so many words, how she felt about him.

And by his warm listening and acceptance, he had told her the same.

Chapter Seven

Wes DuMont announced plans to hold a big dance on Saturday night as a way of introducing more people to the Coaltree Cross-country Express Company. He made arrangements to rent the Crystal Palace for the occasion, and he put out posters advertising the dance as free to all comers.

"Of course I think you should let him use your place," Angus had said when Marybeth asked him about it. "I think a big party would be fun, and if DuMont wants to put one on for the folks, I say let him do it."

Excitement over the event built throughout the week, reaching its peak Saturday morning, when one of the Coaltree coaches arrived carrying the band. Even the children of Casper were excited, and they gathered around the stage depot, laughing, pulling each other's hair, sometimes breaking into a dance of their own. They pretended to be the band, strumming imaginary guitars and playing phantom fiddles and accordions.

The young men of the town—employees of both stage lines, hostlers, and cowboys from the nearby ranches—drifted by casually, as if they had other business to attend to and just happened to be in the area. The young women of the community dropped into the general store, just next door to the new Coaltree depot, to buy brightly colored ribbons or notions, pretending an indifference to the band members, who were at that very moment unloading their instruments.

Amy stood at the door of the Crystal Palace, looking across the street as the four men of the band climbed out and then began taking their instruments down. They realized they were the center of much attention, and they moved importantly, engrossed in the work of unloading, seemingly taking no notice of the excitement their arrival had caused.

"How do they look?" Smith asked, coming up beside her.

Amy smiled and turned toward him. "Why, I would say they are a fine-looking group of musicians. But then you would be a better judge than I."

Smith put his hand above his eyes, assuming the classic pose of a prairie scout. "As fine looking a musical ensemble as I have ever seen," he teased.

Amy laughed. "Will you be attending the festivities tonight?"

"That all depends on whether or not a certain young lady will give me all of her dances."

"All?" Amy said, mischievously questioning his impertinence with her raised eyebrows.

"Well, I won't be greedy. I would be satisfied with three out of every four dances."

"Oh, you're making it easy. I was prepared to give you four out of five."

"You? But I was talking about Miss Pettigrew," Smith teased. "You know the lady, don't you? She's a seamstress for Mrs. Adams."

"Oh, you!" Amy said, shoving him away from her as he began laughing. "Just for that, you'll get no dances from me."

"No, no, I surrender," Smith said, putting his hands up. "I'll take as many dances as you'll let me have. Though I imagine Mr. DuMont will be after you as well."

"Yes, I imagine so," Amy agreed. "And since he's giving the party, I feel that I can hardly say no all the time."

"Smith," Marybeth called from farther back in the room. "Would you help move these tables?"

"Sure," Smith answered, and he walked toward her, giving Amy a wistful nod.

Half a dozen of Angus's employees were clearing out the tables and chairs as they helped to get the Crystal Palace ready, and the whole interior was a beehive of activity.

"Oh, and I'll help Jenny hang the bunting," Amy volunteered.

"Remind you of the cotillions back home?" Smith asked his aunt.

"A little, yes," Marybeth said. "I must confess that I'm looking forward to it, even if it is DuMont's party." She put her hands on her hips and looked around at the busy workers. "I just don't know why we've never done this before."

"Well, let's wait and see how this one goes," Smith proposed. "If nothing goes wrong, maybe we can do it again."

"Don't be silly. What can go wrong at a dance?"

By dusk, excitement over the dance was full-blown. The sound of the practicing musicians, especially the high-skirling fiddle, could be heard all up and down Main Street. Children gathered around the glowing yellow windows and peered inside. The dance floor had been cleared of all tables and chairs, though there were chairs for the nondancers, those too old and those too young, around the perimeter. A platform had been built for the musicians at the front of the room, and bunting of red, white, and blue hung in festoons from the ceiling and draped the walls.

The band started playing even before the dance. They played "The Gandy Dancers' Ball" and "Little Joe the Wrangler." As the horses and buckboards arrived, every hitching rail on the street became full. Men and women streamed along the boardwalks toward the hotel, the women in colorful ginghams, the men in clean blue denims and brightly decorated vests.

Smith was wearing a tan suit and polished boots, with a

dark silk vest covering a white frilled shirt. Compared to most of the other men, he was overdressed, but Amy was glad about it; she had brought out her best dress for the occasion and had been afraid that she might be accused of putting on airs. She was wearing a low-cut dress of gold-colored satin, edged with a lavender ruche and decorated with sprays of dark purple and gold flowers with green leaves. Among her friends in Boston, it would have been just another beautiful dress, but out here it was a sensation, and every woman present came to admire it.

To one side of the dance floor there was a long table with a large punchbowl. Amy watched one of the men walk over to the bowl and unobtrusively pour whiskey into the punch from a bottle he had concealed beneath his vest. A moment later another cowboy did the same thing, and Amy smiled as she thought of the increasing potency of the punch.

The music was playing but as yet no one was dancing. Then the music stopped, and one of the players lifted a megaphone.

"Choose up your squares!" the caller shouted.

The single men made their way toward the unescorted young women. Some of the women giggled shyly; others were more gracious or bold in accepting their invitations. In a moment there were three squares formed and waiting, one of which included Smith and Amy.

The music began, with the fiddles loud and clear, the guitars carrying the rhythm, the accordion providing the counterpoint, and the dobro singing over everything. The caller began to shout, and he clapped his hands and stomped his feet. He danced around on the platform in compliance with his own calls, bowing and whirling as if he had a partner and was in one of the squares himself. The dancers moved and swirled to the caller's commands.

Angus, who was waiting for Marybeth to appear, saw Wes DuMont standing by the wall near the punchbowl. DuMont was watching the dancers, and from the expression on his face, he was not too happy with the fun that

Smith and Amy seemed to be having. Angus went over to talk to him.

"DuMont, on behalf of the town I want to thank you," Angus said. "It's good for them to have something like this to get their mind off everything that's been going on."

DuMont looked at Angus questioningly. "What do you mean by everything that's been going on?"

"The trouble," Angus said. "The murder of Billy, the robbery of one of my coaches, and the attempted robbery of another. And, of course, the mysterious fire."

"Yes, you have been having an unfortunate run of luck, haven't you?"

"If I were a suspicious man, I would wonder why you have been spared," Angus said. "For example, none of your coaches have been robbed, or even approached."

"Yes, but I remind you, Mr. Hightower, that none of my coaches have carried any money. Don't forget, *you* have the specie contracts, not Coaltree."

"I suppose that's true."

"But," DuMont went on, "I am concerned that there are men who think they can just rob a stagecoach with impunity. As soon as I have run you out of business, the money shipments will be going on Coaltree stagecoaches, and I would not like to think of them being robbed."

"In the meantime, it probably doesn't hurt your operation if one of my coaches gets hit every now and then," Angus suggested.

"Mr. Hightower, I'm sorry you feel that way," DuMont said. "I'll tell you what. To prove I'm just as concerned about this as you are, Coaltree Express will offer a five-thousand-dollar reward for the arrest and conviction of the men who robbed your stage."

"You're being awfully generous with Coaltree's money, aren't you?" Angus asked.

"I can afford to be. Mr. Coaltree is a generous man."

"DuMont, why do you want to waste time running me out of business? I'm so small that I cannot possibly represent any threat to Ben Coaltree."

DuMont smiled. "It's obvious, Mr. Hightower, that you have no understanding of business on this high a level."

"I suppose not," Angus admitted.

"Well, please believe me, there is nothing personal in it. Indeed, I rather admire you. The truth is, Mr. Hightower, I wish Coaltree had more people like you. When your stage line shuts down, I'd like you to take over the local operation for us. You'd be doing the same thing you are now, only with Coaltree coaches. You'd be free of worrying about paying salaries, buying stock, or keeping up your equipment."

"Are you speaking for yourself or for Ben Coaltree?"

Dumont smiled broadly. "I intend to succeed here, Mr. Hightower. I also intend to marry Mr. Coaltree's daughter. As his son-in-law, I will have even more authority."

Angus looked over at Amy, who was dancing with Smith. He chuckled. "She may have something to say about that."

DuMont looked toward them. "Are you talking about that piano player?" He smirked as he said, "I hardly think a piano player can be considered a threat."

"DuMont, you said I didn't know anything about big business. Maybe you're right. But if you think that piano player is no threat to your plans for Miss Coaltree, I'd say you don't know a thing about women." Angus chuckled and then walked away, leaving DuMont staring out at the dancers with an expression of bewilderment on his face.

Standing at the back of the room, watching the party but not participating because of his black skin, was Big Troy Lucas. Big Troy did not really want to dance, and there were no ladies of color here for him. There was one back in Omaha, and in another few months when his blacksmith's shop was paid off, Troy was going to bring her out. In the meantime he contented himself with work.

Big Troy looked at the long table loaded down with sliced ham, sliced beef, baked chicken, and cheeses. He would have liked to visit that table, but though no one told him specifically, he knew that the food was as much out of bounds to him as the dancing. He watched as Mr. Meeker moved along the table, filling a plate with an enormous amount of food. Meeker looked up and saw Big Troy watching him, but he did not say a word.

"Big Troy," Smith called just at that moment. The dancers were disbanding with the song's end.

"Yes, suh?"

"What would you like from that table?"

Big Troy smiled. "Well, suh, I don't reckon they's anything on that table I *don't* like."

"I'll get you a plate."

Smith went over to the food table and filled a plate heaping full; then he took it back to the blacksmith. Big Troy thanked him and retreated into a distant corner to eat.

When Smith returned to the dance floor, another tune had started, and he saw that Amy was dancing with DuMont. Amy had mentioned earlier that she felt an obligation to dance at least one dance with DuMont, so Smith was not bothered. Instead he leaned against the wall and watched the swirls of color, listening to the music. When the dance ended, Amy stood in the middle of the floor looking around the room. Smith saw her and raised his hand in a signal. She saw him, smiled, and started in his direction.

"Just a minute!" DuMont called after her. "Where do you think you're going?"

Startled by DuMont's call, Amy stopped and looked back toward him. "I beg your pardon?" she said.

Smith started toward Amy and reached her at about the same time as DuMont.

"I've been very patient with you and this . . . this piano player," DuMont said, twisting the last words to sound like a derisive epithet. "But my patience has a limit. You'll not be dancing any more dances with him tonight."

Amy's mouth dropped open in amazement for a moment before she said, "Mr. DuMont, you have no right to be patient or impatient with me. The men I dance with are my own business, and if I choose to dance with Smith again, I shall do so."

"But he's a cheap piano player in a tawdry saloon. Don't you understand? He isn't our kind."

"*Our* kind? How do you presume to include me in such a statement? I don't know what *your* kind is." Amy's eyes blazed indignantly.

"I'm executive secretary to your father," DuMont said. "As such, I feel responsible for you until he arrives."

"DuMont, Miss Coaltree is quite capable of being responsible for herself," Smith said.

"You stay out of it, piano player," DuMont said.

"I don't believe Miss Coaltree wants me out of it," Smith replied. "In fact, I believe that if there's anyone she wants out of her life, it's you."

The color rose in DuMont's face. "Take that back," he demanded.

"Come on, Amy, let's go for a walk until he cools down," Smith suggested. He was reaching for Amy's hand when suddenly he felt an explosion on the side of his head. He saw bright lights and felt his knees buckle. The next thing he knew he was lying down, looking up at DuMont, who was standing over him with his arm cocked and his hand made into a fist.

"Get up!" DuMont said, smiling insanely. "Get up, so I can knock you down again."

Smith was dizzy and his ears were ringing, but he tried to get up. He had gotten only to his knees when DuMont sent a whistling right smashing into his face, and he went down again. DuMont began to kick him in the side.

"Stop it!" Amy screamed. "Stop it! You'll kill him!"

Smith had never been much of a brawler. He had avoided fights when he was a boy because he had always been afraid of injuring his hands. His fights as an adult had been with a gun, swift and permanent. DuMont, on the other hand, had fought and scrapped his way through life, beginning in the orphanage. The edge was clearly his, and he was taking full advantage of it.

By now, much of the other activity in the room had ceased as more and more of the guests realized what was happening. When Marybeth became aware of the fight, she rushed to pull DuMont away from Smith, only to be flung back into the growing crowd. After catching her breath, she went in search of Angus.

Seeing how Marybeth had been treated, a townsman stepped in to reprimand DuMont and to offer Smith some assistance, but as soon as he made a move toward Du-Mont, the huge bodyguard named Meeker lumbered up to him, and the townsman backed off.

Smith managed to get to his feet, but he stood there unsteadily as DuMont circled. DuMont grew overconfident and waded in for the kill. As he did so he dropped his guard, and Smith managed to slip in a quick, solid blow to DuMont's nose, which crunched under his fist. Bright red blood flowed down DuMont's mouth and over his chin.

Smith grinned in triumph, but his triumph was short-lived. DuMont came back with a delayed counterpunch and caught Smith high on the temple with a stunning blow. Another split the skin on his cheekbones.

Smith tried to fight back, but DuMont was too much for him. He reeled backward under a rain of blows, and once again he went down. He tried to summon the strength to get back onto his feet, but his knees felt weak as water, and there was no strength in his arms. The toe of Du-Mont's boot caught him in the side again, and he was spun over onto his back. The pain in his ribs was like a knife thrust.

A succession of kicks landed on his head and sides. By now he was numb and feeling little pain. His consciousness was fading. He ceased trying to struggle, instead curling into a fetal position, keeping his forearms around his head.

Just before blackness finally claimed him, he heard Amy pleading for someone to help him.

Several of the townspeople intervened then, and half a

dozen men closed in on DuMont. They grabbed him and pulled him away from Smith's prostrate form.

"Mister," one of them said angrily, "the piano player may be a dandy, but by God he's *our* dandy. If you've hurt his hands so he can't play no more, we're gonna break both your arms."

The warning was no sooner out of the cowboy's mouth than half a dozen Coaltree employees swooped down on him and the other men who had come to Smith's rescue. With that, a knockdown, drag-out brawl began, with men rushing in from all sides, and screaming women running to get out of the way. One brawler was thrown onto the stage, and the band, who had already stopped the music, now decided that the better part of valor dictated that they get out of there. Holding their instruments over their heads to protect them, they scurried to one side of the room.

Another brawler climbed up onto the punchbowl table, ran down its entire length, and then leaped, belly first, into the fray. A moment later, when the punchbowl table was overturned, the bowl shattered, and the strong, alcoholic smell of the punch permeated the area.

Fred, the bartender, hurried behind the bar and turned the crank to draw the crystal chandelier as high up out of the way as he could. Marybeth breathed a sigh of relief as she saw it lift up just in time to avoid a thrown chair.

The chair that missed the chandelier did not miss the front window, however, and there was a loud, crashing noise as it exploded. One of the brawlers followed the chair through the window, and soon people began to pour out into the street. For that Marybeth was grateful, because as more went into the street, fewer were left inside to do any greater damage to her place.

Meeker, who would have sided with the Coaltree employees, and Big Troy, who surely would have sided with the citizens of the town, stayed out of the fight. They watched the brawl, and each other, but neither made a motion to get involved.

When it looked as if the fight was about to lose its momentum and break up, the sheriff and Angus worked together to slow the action further by pulling people apart and shoving them aside. Finally the fighting came to a complete halt, and men stood around on the boardwalk or out in the middle of the street, their clothes soiled by dirt, blood, and horse droppings, looking on sheepishly at what they had done.

"I hope you men feel proud of yourselves," the sheriff said angrily. He turned his hat upside down and put it on the edge of the boardwalk. "Now I think a few of you better start dropping some money into this hat so we can make up a fund to pay for the damage you've caused to Marybeth's place."

"No need for that, Sheriff," DuMont said. "Coaltree Cross-country Express will pay for all the damage."

DuMont was holding a handkerchief to his nose. The bleeding had stopped, but his nose was visibly swollen, perhaps fractured. He walked back into the Crystal Palace, where he saw Amy, Marybeth, and Big Troy kneeling beside Smith. Smith was conscious now, and his head was resting in Marybeth's lap.

"I'm sorry about this," DuMont apologized. He pointed toward Smith. "But the piano player was just asking for somebody to teach him a lesson."

"Get away from us, Mr. DuMont," Amy said angrily. "You just get away and stay away."

Big Troy helped Smith to his feet. Moving on shaky legs, and supported by Big Troy, Smith started to his room. Amy went with them, and Marybeth hurried ahead to turn down the bed.

In the room, Marybeth poured water into the basin; then she and Amy started tending to the cuts and bruises Smith had sustained.

"Oh, Smith," Amy said, nearly in tears. "Oh, how could DuMont have done such a thing? If he has hurt your hands . . ." She sighed, letting the sentence hang.

Smith made a grunting sound that might have been a

chuckle. One eye was puffed closed and both his lips were split, but his features arranged themselves into something of a smile.

"Don't worry about my hands," he said. "They are fine." He flexed his fingers but then winced as she began treating a cut under his eye.

"You could have been badly hurt," Amy said. "You're hurt badly enough now, but it could have been even more serious."

"I guess I'm not much of a fighter," Smith said.

"Please, don't apologize to me," Amy said. "Believe me, I am not impressed by someone who is a brawler."

"Well," Smith said, attempting another smile, "then you should certainly be impressed by me, because I'm just the opposite. As Aunt Marybeth can tell you, I wasn't a fighter, even as a child."

Amy looked up at the older woman in surprise.

"You . . . you are his aunt?"

"Yes," Marybeth said. "And he's right, he was always a good boy who never fought or gave his mother, my sister, a difficult time."

"I was always too busy practicing the piano," Smith said.

"He studied in Rome, under Franz Liszt, you know," Marybeth said proudly. "And he made the grand tour, playing in all the capitals of Europe."

"I *knew* it," Amy said. "I knew you were something special."

"Oh, yes," Smith said. "I'm something special all right. Most people go ahead as their lives progress. . . . I, on the other hand, have gone backward. From the Paris opera house to a drink-stained piano in a Casper saloon."

"We'd better let you rest now," Amy said, realizing that she had just glimpsed a part of the mystery of this man, and not wanting to pressure him to reveal more until he was in a better frame of mind. She stood up and looked down at him. "I'll check on you again later, if you don't mind."

"You can look in on me anytime," Smith said.

Big Troy hung back for a moment until Amy and Marybeth were both gone. Smith closed his eyes, but sensing that someone was still there, he opened them again. "Big Troy, you still around?"

"Yes, suh. Do you be sick at your stomach?"

"Sick at my stomach? No, I don't think so. I hurt all over, but I'm not sick. Why?"

"When a prizefighter gets beat up bad like you just done, they can mos' generally get over it pretty good iffen they don't get sick at the stomach. When they get sick at the stomach, it means they's hurt bad. You ain't sick, and that's a good sign."

Smith chuckled. "I'm gratified to know that something about my condition is good," he said. He turned to look at Big Troy through the eye that was still open. "I saw you and Mr. Meeker looking each other over."

"Yes, suh. When I was a prizefighter, I had a chance to fight that gennel'man," Big Troy said. "But his manager wouldn't put up his belt 'cause I was colored."

"You think you will fight him?"

"Yes, suh, I expects I will."

"Why?"

"Mr. Smith, they's some things that's just meant to happen," Big Troy answered. "Me fightin' Mr. Meeker is one. You fightin' the albino is another."

Smith looked at Big Troy with shock. "What . . . what makes you say that?"

"You're Mr. Butler, ain't you? Captain Rufus Butler?"

Smith let out a long sigh. "How'd you know?"

"Me an' you met before, Mr. Butler. Does you recollect the town of Coffeyville?"

Smith closed his eyes for a moment, and he remembered the flames and smelled the smoke of a dozen burning buildings. Women and children were huddled together in a plaza in the center of the town, looking out of terror-filled eyes at the guerrillas from Quantrill's band ransacking the buildings.

One of the guerrillas had a big black man at the end of a rope, and he was firing his pistol at the black man's feet.

"Dance, nigger!" he was shouting. He fired again, and the bullet hit the dirt, kicking up dust. The black man stood still.

"Dance, nigger! I like to see niggers dance, an' the bigger they are, the better I like it." He fired again, and this time his bullet nicked the black man's leg. The black man's pants stained quickly with blood, but he stood there as motionless as before.

"Damn you, nigger, if you don't dance this time, I'm gonna put a bullet in your woolly skull."

"Fitch!" Captain Rufus Butler called to him when he saw what was going on. "What the hell are you doing?"

"I'm just havin' a little fun with this here nigger is all."

"I've got an idea that might be even more fun," Butler said.

"What's that?" Fitch asked, laughing obscenely. He looked over at the women and children. "Somethin' to do with the women?"

"No. Something to do with guns. Suppose you put your pistol in your holster, and I put my pistol in my holster, and then we draw against each other. Whoever wins can kill the other one."

"What? That's crazy. You know I can't outdraw you."

"Then you're going to die."

"No . . . you're crazy . . . I don't want to do that."

"Then you leave this man alone."

Fitch looked at the big black man and then laughed nervously.

"Why, sure, Captain. Whyn't you tell me you was a nigger lover? I wouldn't have done nothin' to him at all if I'd have known that."

"Does you recollect?" Big Troy asked, bringing Smith back to the present.

"The colored man in the town plaza," Smith said.

"Yes, suh. I was the colored man, and you was the one stopped that soldier. You was Captain Rufus Butler then."

"Who else knows who I am?" Smith asked.

"Far as I know, they don't no one else know," Big Troy said. "I figure you got a reason for not wantin' no one to know, and whatever that reason is, it's good enough for me. I ain't told a soul."

"Thanks, Big Troy."

Big Troy walked over to the bed and put his huge hand on Smith's shoulder.

"No, suh, Mr. Smith. I reckon it's about time I got around to thankin' you."

Chapter Eight

Payson stood on the rock overhang, looking down into the valley two thousand feet below. There, just coming off the valley floor and starting up the winding mountain road, was the Wyoming Rapid Express afternoon stage. From this distance it was so tiny it looked like some sort of insect crawling along the ground.

Payson turned to look back at the two men who were with him. The tall redhead was Keefer; the shorter, dark-haired man was Monroe. Monroe was lying down, his head on a rock, his hat pulled down over his eyes. Keefer was sitting nearby, whittling on a stick with his bone-handled hunting knife.

Keefer glanced up and saw that Payson was looking toward them. "Did you see the stage?" he asked.

"Yes," Payson hissed unpleasantly.

"Look like it's carrying the money?"

"How the hell am I supposed to know from up here?" Payson replied. He walked over to the remains of their campfire and poured himself a cup of coffee. It would be a long, exhausting climb for the team, and he knew the driver would halt the horses at the turnout to let the animals rest. The driver would also stop to check the brakes before the descent down the other side, allowing the passengers time to "stretch their legs," a gentle euphemism for walking into the woods to relieve themselves.

"Payson, what say if the stage is carryin' the money, we just take it an' skedaddle on outta here?" Keefer suggested. "There don't seem to be no need in stayin' around here much longer."

Payson didn't answer. Instead, he just took a swallow of his coffee and stared at Keefer through his cold eyes.

Keefer cleared his throat. "I mean, what good is it havin' the money iffen we can't spend none of it? An' there sure ain't no way we can stay around here an' spend it without people knowin' we was the ones what robbed the stage in the first place. Besides which, if people keep on accusin' us, the sheriff is finally gonna start listenin'."

"The sheriff stays alive only as long as the sheriff stays deaf," Payson said. "He knows that for certain, so we aren't going to have any trouble."

"But the sheriff ain't the only one around here. There's always the chance a vigilante committee could get started up, an' I've seen them vigilantes work before."

"Have you?" Payson asked in a scornful tone.

"Yes, sir, I have. Back in Kansas there was a group got formed up an' they commenced to hangin' an' shootin' everyone in sight. They didn't bother with no trials or nothin' like that. Fact is, they didn't even round up folks for a particular crime. They just rounded up everyone they ever heard had rode a crooked trail."

"You let me worry about the vigilantes," Payson said.

Payson carried his cup back to the rock overhang and looked down toward the stage. He knew it would be at least half an hour before the stage would be at the turnout. Sipping his coffee, he thought back to a time in Texas, five years earlier, when he had been a part of a vigilante posse.

Sweet Thompson, a cowhand for the Lazy-L, had been murdered, and two dozen Lazy-L cows had disappeared. The owner of the Lazy-L had not yet returned from Amarillo, and the sheriff was in Dumas, so the good citizens of Middle Water formed a vigilante committee to go after the murderers and recover the cattle.

Payson had lived in Middle Water, working at the livery stable. He was a loner, a condition originally forced on him because of his white hair, pale skin, and otherworldly eyes. His physical appearance frightened children and put off all but the hardiest women. But despite his being neither well known nor well liked, everyone knew that when he was not working at the livery stable, he was practicing with his guns. They also knew how good he was, and no one wanted to cross him. Given his talent with guns, it was only natural that on the day the vigilante committee was formed, a delegation of Middle Water citizens came to the livery stable and asked him to lead them.

When Payson and the angry vigilantes caught up with the missing cattle that night, they found three men nearby, leisurely eating their supper. Payson questioned the three men. The youngest was eighteen, the middle-aged man was the boy's father, and the oldest was his grandfather. They claimed they had bought the cows from the Lazy-L owner early that morning and were taking them back to their own ranch. They also claimed they knew nothing about Sweet Thompson's being killed.

"We got a bill of sale," the grandfather had insisted.

"A bill of sale can be made up," Payson had replied. "I say we got the right people. Come on, let's string them up."

When one of the vigilantes protested, saying the three men should be taken to the sheriff, an argument ensued, resulting in Payson hotheadedly pulling his gun and shooting the vigilante. The rest of the riders, not wanting Payson's wrath to fall upon them, went along with him then, and the three men were hanged.

The vigilantes had just cut the bodies down when the owner of the Lazy-L rode up, saying that the killer of Sweet Thompson had turned himself in. When he saw the three bodies, his face blanched. He had sold the nearby cattle to the three dead men earlier that day, he explained.

Payson, now draining his coffee cup, remembered what had happened next. The friends of the vigilante he had shot had wanted to hang the albino then and there, but he had pulled his gun on them and said he was leaving, threatening to kill anyone who followed him. That had been the beginning of his life as Fast Charlie Payson, outlaw gunslinger.

Payson turned away from the edge of the overlook, and the pictures from his past dissolved. He was here, with Keefer and Monroe, waiting to rob the Wyoming Rapid Express.

"Get Monroe up," he growled. "The stage will be here in a few minutes."

Keefer kicked Monroe on the bottom of his feet, and the other man tipped his hat back, stood up, and walked over to his horse. The three men put on long, yellow dusters, tying bandannas around the bottom half of their faces.

Once they were mounted, they rode over to a stand of trees near the turnout and waited for the stage. It arrived a moment later, the horses snorting with fatigue and straining into the harness.

"Whoa! Hold it up there, team," the driver called out. Then he spoke to his passengers, telling them to get out and stretch their legs, if they wished.

At that instant, Payson rode out into the road in front of the stage. The driver and shotgun guard started in surprise, and the guard slowly began reaching for his shotgun.

"Don't do it, unless you want to die," Payson warned him. The guard drew his hand back. "You folks in the stage, now, go ahead and do like the driver said."

Four people left the stage, two men and two women. One man was obviously a farmer, and as far as Payson could tell, unarmed. The other was small and mousey looking, the type usually found keeping books in drygoods stores. The two women appeared to be the only kind Payson knew well, referred to by some as soiled doves.

Keefer started toward the passengers.

"Leave 'em be," Payson hissed. "Whatever they got they can keep. All we want is the money that's in the strongbox."

"You heard the man," Keefer growled at the driver.

"Take the money out from under the seat and throw it down."

"What makes you think there's any money in the box?" the driver challenged.

"Just do it," Payson ordered.

The driver reached under the seat. He hesitated for a moment, and Payson knew he was thinking about going for a gun. Payson cocked his pistol, and the metallic sounds of the cylinder turning and the hammer locking into place were loud and frightening.

"Driver, you may have less than a second to live."

Quickly the driver opened the box, took out the money sack, and held it up so Payson could see that he had it. Then he tossed it over the side.

"Very good," Payson said. "Now, any of you folks gotta relieve yourselves, you go right ahead and do it."

"There are ladies present," the mousey store clerk said.

"You think women don't pee?" Payson asked. The two soiled doves tittered in amusement, but no one moved.

Keefer hoisted up the money sack and let out a low whistle. "You was right," he said. "This is full of money."

Payson tossed his saddlebag down. "Fill this," he ordered.

Happily, Keefer began stuffing bills into the pouches. Finally, when both sides were bulging, he handed the sack back up to the albino. Payson draped it across the saddle in front of him.

"Driver, it looks like nobody has to water the lilies, so why don't you get 'em back on board and get on outta here?"

"Climb aboard, folks," the driver ordered.

When the four passengers had climbed onto the stage, the driver whistled at his team and snapped the whip, and the horses responded. A moment later the stage was rolling downhill toward Casper, while Payson and his two partners rode away in the opposite direction.

Angus, Marybeth, and Amy were sitting at Angus's table in the Crystal Palace. Smith, one eye still discolored and a scar healing on his cheek, was playing the piano. Angus was reading *Harper's Weekly*.

"Listen to this," he chuckled. "This is a joke from 'Humors of the Day.'" Clearing his throat, he began to read. "An English gentleman once fell from his horse and injured his thumb. The pain increasing, he was obliged to send for a surgeon. One day the doctor was unable to visit his patient, and therefore sent his son instead. 'Have you visited the Englishman?' said his father in the evening. 'Yes,' replied the young man. 'And I have drawn out a thorn, which I ascertained to be the chief cause of his agony.' 'Fool!' exclaimed the father. 'I trusted you had more sense; now there is an end to the job!'"

Angus guffawed loudly, and Marybeth and Amy laughed, though more at Angus's appreciation of the story than at the story itself.

In the middle of the laugh, Marybeth saw Deekus step through the front door. She waved at him, and as he walked toward their table, said, "Deekus, won't you join us? Angus is entertaining us with jokes from the newspaper."

"Thank you, Miss Staley," Deekus said. "But this ain't no social call. Boss, I just seen the stage across the river, and it's comin' hell-for-leather. I figure that ain't a very good sign."

Angus folded the paper and laid it on the table. "All right, I'll be right out," he said. "Thanks, Deekus."

Smith stopped playing and looked over toward their table. "Trouble?" he inquired.

Angus ran his hand nervously through his hair.

"Yeah," he said. "I didn't let word out because I hoped I could sneak it through. But the money shipment for Fort Fetterman that was supposed to come tomorrow was on today's stage."

"Oh, Angus, how much was it?" Marybeth asked.

"According to the wire I got, it was supposed to be more than fifteen thousand," Angus said.

Smith let out a whistle. "That's a lot of money," he said.

"Yeah," Angus agreed. He stood up. "I guess I better go out and meet it."

*   *   *

It was not normal for the afternoon stage to arrive with the team in full gallop, so everyone in town knew that something out of the ordinary had happened. Therefore, when the stage slid to a stop in front of the Crystal Palace, with the driver pushing on the brake lever and hauling back on the reins, a score or more people stood on the boardwalk or in the street to see what was going on. The wheels and bottom of the coach still dripped water from fording the river at the edge of town, and the horses' sides were heaving mightily as they regained their breath.

"Eb, you want to tell me what this is all about?" Angus asked.

"We was robbed," the driver answered.

The sheriff arrived just in time to hear the announcement. "Another holdup?" he asked.

"Afraid so," Angus answered.

"This is getting to be a habit with your coaches, isn't it, Angus?"

"Maybe if you'd catch the robbers, it wouldn't be so common!" Angus retorted.

"I can't catch them if I don't know who they are."

"Hell, Sheriff, you know damn well who they are. Tell him, Eb. Tell him who held you up."

"I don't know who it was, Angus," Eb said, looking away nervously. "They was wearin' masks and dusters."

"Carl?" Angus asked the guard. "Did you get a look at them?"

"Not so's I could tell who they were," Carl said. He, like Eb, refused to look Angus in the eye when he spoke.

The passengers were out of the coach now, and everyone gathered around them to get their impressions.

"There was three of 'em," the farmer said. "The leader had funny-lookin' eyes. Can't quite put my finger on it."

"What color were they?"

"Well, I don't rightly know," the farmer said. "His eyebrows was white though, I can tell you that."

"The other two men," Angus said. "One was redheaded, the other dark?"

The farmer stroked his jaw for a moment. "Near as I can recollect, that description would fit 'em," he said.

"Sheriff, that's Payson, Keefer, and Monroe," Angus said.

"How about you others?" the sheriff asked. "You got anything to say? Do you agree with this man about the descriptions?"

"I do, it was . . ." the clerk started to say, but his wife, who met him at the stage, cut him off with one word— "Elmer!"

"I'm telling the sheriff about the men who robbed us," Elmer explained.

"You want to get us shot?" his wife asked in a loud whisper. "Maybe you don't care about yourself, but what about me and the baby? You want those robbers to murder us in our beds?"

"Why, no . . . no, of course not," Elmer said.

"Then you didn't see anything," she said.

The sheriff sighed and then turned to the two women. "What about you two?" he asked. "I'll wager you've seen enough men in your profession. You ever see any of these men before?"

"Sheriff, if the driver and shotgun guard ain't gonna tell you nothin', what makes you think we will?" one of the women asked.

"Besides," the other one put in, "they didn't take nothin' from us. All they got was the money shipment."

The sheriff shook his head and turned to Angus. "You want to go on with this?" he asked.

"No, I reckon not," he said. Shaking with anger and frustration, he turned and walked back into the Crystal Palace.

It was nearly an hour later that the driver and shotgun guard came into the saloon. By now the horses were unharnessed and cared for, and the coach had been readied for the early turnaround the next morning. They approached the table where Angus and Marybeth sat, and stood there sheepishly.

"Sit down, Eb, Carl," Angus said. "What do you want to drink?"

"Beer," Eb said.

"Me, too," added Carl.

Angus signaled Fred for two beers, and a moment later the mugs were set before the driver and guard. They both took long, satisfying drinks.

"That's good," Eb said. He wiped the foam from his lips with the back of his hand. "Angus . . ."

"I know," Angus interrupted, "you're going to tell me that you recognized the holdup men."

"Yeah," Eb said. "It was who you said it was . . . the albino and them two that runs with him all the time. They had on dusters, hats, masks, but there ain't no way that son of a bitch can hide who he is." Eb touched the brim of his hat. "Beg pardon 'bout the language, ma'am," he said to Marybeth.

"Never mind about the language," Marybeth said. "Why didn't you tell the sheriff what you just told us?"

"Miss Staley, I got me a wife and four kids," Eb said. "The wife figures drivin' a stage is dangerous enough, what with ever' other one bein' held up an' all. I don't plan on makin' her a widow 'cause I gotta open my big mouth. Yeah, it was the albino all right, but I seen what happened to Billy, an' I ain't gonna let that happen to me."

"I reckon that goes for me as well," Carl said.

"Angus, if you don't want me drivin' for you no more 'cause of that, well, I reckon I'll understand. I just hope you understand why it's gotta be this way."

"Angus, you ain't got no wife an' kids," Carl went on. "If you did, you'd see right off what we're talkin' about."

"I do see what you're talking about," Angus said. "And as for not working for me anymore, don't be silly. You two men have a job as long as I have a company." Angus sighed. "The problem is, if this goes on much longer, I'm not going to have a company."

"What are you going to do now, Angus?" Marybeth asked.

"I'm going to go have a conversation with Wesley Du-Mont," Angus answered.

Wesley DuMont sat behind his desk in the new office. Before him was a ledger book, and in it was an accounting of everything that had been spent so far. There was also a column denoting how much money he had left. The amount of money expended nearly matched the remaining money.

At this rate, DuMont figured he had only nine days left. Nine more days, and he would be completely out of money. Nine days to break Angus Hightower, or be broken himself. If he failed, he would face Ben Coaltree in disgrace.

No, he told himself. That was not going to happen. He was not going to face Ben Coaltree in disgrace. He had never failed before, and he had no intention of failing now.

DuMont thought back to a time long ago. He was twelve years old and had been in the orphanage for as long as he could remember. All he knew of his background was that he was a foundling, that he had been left on the doorstep of the orphanage with a note from the unwed woman who was his mother. He was a bastard, and over the years he had been called that many times. He could not change the circumstances of his birth, but he certainly intended to change the circumstances of his life.

DuMont studied hard in school. He was a very good student who made excellent grades. While boys who studied hard and made good grades were often popular with their teachers, he was not. His ambition was obsessive, and he would go to any extreme to get ahead. He was mean-spirited and selfish, did not make friends, and was often cruel to those who were younger and weaker. He expected the highest standards of performance from everyone, especially himself. He would do whatever it took to keep from failing, and that thought brought him back to the immediate tasks at hand.

DuMont pulled an envelope from one of the cubbyholes of his desk, put ten dollars in it, and wrote the name of the telegrapher on the outside. He gave the envelope to his station manager, Blair Morann. "I owe this money to the Western Union office," he said. "Please, deliver it for me."

"All right," Morann replied, taking the envelope. The man started out the door, but then he stopped and turned around. "Mr. DuMont, you got company comin'. Angus Hightower."

"Show him in, show him in," DuMont said. He had heard of Hightower's bad luck again today. Maybe Hightower was coming to give up.

But DuMont soon learned that Angus was not there to give up; he was there to ask for help.

"You want help?" At first DuMont was not sure what to think.

"Yes," Angus assured him. "I believed you the other night when you told me you were as concerned with these robberies as I am."

"I am concerned. I truly am," DuMont said. "And I've been giving some thought to the problem. I have a solution if you are willing to listen."

"I'll listen to any proposal," Angus said.

"All right, here it is. Your coaches are being hit because the highwaymen know that they are the only ones carrying large amounts of money. Suppose you transship some of that money through me?"

"You're asking me to give up my money shipments?"

"No, not give them up. You are still the main carrier for the fort, the bank, and the telegraph office, and I'll give you a percentage of every shipment I carry. But with both lines carrying money, the robbers won't have any idea which stage to rob."

Angus thought for a moment and then shook his head.

"No," he said. "Mind you, your idea does have some merit. But how would it look to my customers if I admitted that I couldn't guarantee the safety of their money shipments? I think I'd better continue to carry them myself . . . at least for as long as I stay in business. No, I have another idea I want to try."

"What is that?"

"I would like to organize a vigilante committee, made up of men from both stage lines. We could have the committee patrol the roads, and the next time one of my stages is hit, the vigilantes would go after the thieves."

DuMont thought about it for a moment and then shook his head.

"I want to help, Hightower, but I don't think Mr. Coaltree would like my forming a vigilante committee from his employees. Vigilante committees have a way of getting nasty. They don't always follow the law."

"This committee would be completely legal," Angus insisted. "I'd get the sheriff to deputize all the men."

"No, I'm afraid not. However, my offer to carry your money shipments still stands, as does my willingness to pay five thousand dollars for Payson's arrest and conviction."

"As frightened as everyone is of the albino right now," Angus said with unmasked sarcasm in his voice, "I'd say your five thousand dollars is pretty safe."

Chapter Nine

Desperate to bring Wyoming Rapid Express to its knees, Wes DuMont began taking extreme measures to ensure his success. He brought in two additional strings of horses that week and hired more hostlers. He then rented all the available space in the livery stable, so that Angus's teams, which normally had free run of the stable, were squeezed into a tight corner. He bought every sack of feed available in Casper, thereby forcing Angus to bring in oats by wagon from Medicine Bow, just to feed his animals. On top of that, DuMont lowered his fares so that two could ride for the price of one, and even those regular passengers who had been most loyal to Angus were unable to resist such a bargain. As a result, the Coaltree stages were making every trip with a full load, while Angus's stages were running virtually empty.

To Angus's employees, the handwriting was on the wall. If there was no business, there would be no money, and if there was no money, there would be no jobs. The same thing was evident to the Coaltree men, for they realized if Coaltree Cross-country was unsuccessful in taking over the business, their own jobs were at risk.

What had started as a clash of businessmen had become a very personal battle between the ordinary citizens of Casper. Men and families who had been friends before, now found themselves in opposite camps, and hard feelings began to build.

There was an unspoken division of territory. Those who

worked for or backed Coaltree Cross-country Express frequented certain saloons in town, notably the Angry Bull, while those who supported Angus gathered at other watering holes, primarily the Crystal Palace. The battle lines even extended to church that Sunday. The Coaltree men and their families sat on the left, the Wyoming Rapid Express men and their families sat on the right. Parson MacAlister tried to be fair, looking first at one side then at the other in equal measure, wishing he could recapture the persuasive magic that he had felt in his sermon at Billy Sinclair's funeral, but to no avail. The congregation filed into and out of church in stony, unchristian silence. Women withdrew from the garden and tea clubs, and quilting bees were canceled. In the schoolyard and around the swimming hole, fights broke out among the children, the sides drawn up along company lines.

Casper had become a town divided.

The piano was playing merrily in the Angry Bull, but the piano player there ran a poor second to Smith. Even the uneducated ears of the cowboys could tell the difference, but tonight it did not matter, because no one was listening. Wes DuMont had just made his first payroll, and all of his employees were celebrating. The noise was such that no one could hear the piano from more than ten feet away.

In one corner some of the men had started their own singing in competition with the piano, while in another corner one of DuMont's drivers, quite drunk, was giving his interpretation of the Mexican hat dance.

Wes DuMont was not present for the celebration, but Blair Morann was. Morann was standing at the bar watching the festivities. The dancing driver was Crack Kendall, and Crack was jumping around, stomping his feet close to the sweat-stained hat he had thrown on the floor.

"Hey, Blair," someone called. "If you don't watch Crack, he's gonna quit drivin' the stage and become a fandango dancer."

"He'll never make it." Morann laughed. "He can't dance any better'n he can drive a team."

"Oh, yeah?" Crack called. "Well, just watch this step."

Crack jumped up and attempted to click his heels together. His feet became entangled, and he fell to the floor in a heap. His fall was greeted with loud laughter, and someone tossed him a bottle of whiskey. Though failed as a dancer, Crack salvaged some of his pride as an exhibitionist by adroitly catching the bottle, turning it up with a flourish, and taking several deep swallows while still seated on the floor.

The saloon doors swung open and several more men entered. These were some of Angus's employees, and they moved sullenly to the far end of the bar.

"Well, now," Crack called when he saw the men enter. "Lookie here, who we have. You fellas are in the wrong place, aren't you? Don't you belong across the street in the Crystal Palace?"

"Yeah, with your boss and his sweet-cake woman."

"And that fancy-pants piano player."

"Hey, Deekus, I got a question for you," Crack called to one of the newcomers. "What you gonna do for a livin' after Hightower goes broke?" Crack laughed loudly, and the others laughed with him.

"Say, I gotta good idea," one of the other Coaltree men said, joining in the spirit of things. "They could all come down to the stable and shovel horseshit. What with all the horses we bought, there's plenty enough to keep 'em all busy." The suggestion was met with an explosion of laughter, but one of Angus's employees, unamused by the joke, threw his beer mug. That was all it took to start the fight.

"Seventy-five dollars?" Angus asked.

"And fifty cents," the sheriff answered. "That's your men's share of the damages to the Angry Bull."

Grumbling, Angus paid the bill. He looked back in the cell and saw half a dozen of his men, bruised and cut from the fight. "I ought to let you all stay in there," he said to them in exasperation.

"Angus, maybe you better see if you can do something about this," the sheriff said. "The situation between the Coaltree Express employees and your men is heating up pretty good. I'm afraid it might get out of hand."

"Well, it isn't surprising," Angus said. "When all this is over, there's going to be only one stage line left. That means about half these fellas are going to be out of work."

"Wish it didn't have to be that-way," the sheriff said. "It sure would make my job a lot easier if everyone could just get along."

Angus stood by the sheriff's desk as his men were released from the cell. One by one they filed by Angus, looking sheepishly at the floor as they passed him. Their hats were hanging on hooks by the door, and as they reached for them, Angus saw Deekus among the men.

"Deekus, you're too old for such nonsense," Angus scolded.

"I reckon I am, boss," Deekus said. "But it galls a man to stand around and watch the company he's been loyal to get knocked down. I just couldn't take it no more."

There was a twinkle in Angus's eyes as he walked over and put his hand on the tough old driver's shoulder. "I just have one question," Angus asked with a chuckle.

"What's that?"

"Did you get one for me?"

Deekus smiled broadly. "I'm not sure which," he said. "But I think I changed the shape of one of 'em's nose."

"Yeah, it was mine, you wrinkled old bastard," Crack called from his cell. And all of Angus's men laughed as they filed out the door.

There was another fight later that night, and another the next day. Though neither incident required Angus to put up more money for damages, the complexion of the fighting had changed. No longer were the fights just between workingmen of both lines. Wes DuMont had hired three men who, Angus was certain, had never done an honest day's work in their lives. They were little more than thugs, men adept at barroom brawling. Not content to wait until fights broke out of their own accord, the three bullies went out of their way to pick fights, and the next night two of Angus's men, badly beaten, quit their jobs.

"We're workin' men, Mr. Hightower," one of them told him reluctantly. Both of them, with swollen and discolored faces, one with his arm in a sling, were standing by Angus's table in the Crystal Palace.

"Yes, sir," the other one added. "We don't mind gettin' into a little fight every now and again, and I figure we can hold our own with others that's just like us. But when DuMont goes to hirin' brawlers, why, that's a little more than we want to get into."

"I hope us quittin' like this don't upset you too much, Mr. Hightower. We ain't never worked for no man better'n you."

"No, sir. Nor your equal neither," the other added. "But there comes a time when a man's gotta look out for hisself."

"And if things ever calm down an' you're willin' to take us back, we'd like to come work for you again."

"It's all right," Angus said. "I understand, and I don't hold it against you. Where will you be going now?"

"Somewhere where a man can work without havin' to get his head bashed in," one replied, the other nodding his agreement.

"I'd be glad to write letters for both of you," Angus said.

"Thanks, Mr. Hightower. We knew you'd take it good."

When both men had left the Crystal Palace, Angus looked across the table at Smith, who had interrupted his playing a few minutes earlier to join Angus for a drink.

"I don't know, Smith," Angus said. "Maybe I'm just fooling myself. Maybe the best thing is to go ahead and give in to Coaltree."

"It isn't Coaltree you'd be giving in to," Smith said.

Angus looked at him in surprise. "What do you mean?"

"I don't know this fella Coaltree," Smith said. "But I'd be willing to bet anything you want to bet that he has no idea what DuMont is doing here, in his name. You ask me, a letter to Coaltree might set things straight."

"I don't know," Angus said. "Ben Coaltree isn't known as a man who gets involved in the small details."

"Maybe not," Smith said. "But Ben Coaltree is Amy's father. I've always thought blood would tell, and Amy's got good feelings and good instincts. She may never have seen her father, but it's his blood in her veins, and that more than likely means that he has good instincts, too."

"You think I should write Coaltree a letter? Is that what you're saying?"

"Yes."

Angus smiled broadly. "I just might do that," he said. He stood up. "In the meantime, it might not hurt to pay another visit to DuMont. I still think he's a man I can reason with."

"You have more kindly thoughts about the son of a bitch than I do," Smith said. "But I wish you luck."

As Angus left the Crystal Palace, Fast Charlie Payson was across the street in the Angry Bull. He was standing just inside the door, drinking a beer, and he watched Angus walk down the street toward the Coaltree office. Payson had to admit he enjoyed the sight of two "respectable" businessmen fighting it out. Their bickering with each other had opened up great opportunities for him, and he had no intention of leaving Casper until he had picked the bones clean.

Payson thought of the piano player in the Crystal Palace, the one they called Smith—the one he had come upon riding with the Coaltree woman that day. There was something about Smith, something that was just out of reach, like a dream he could not remember. There was something not quite right about him, and Payson thought it was time to set it straight. He finished the beer, put the glass on the table beside him, and pushed open the door.

"Hey, Fast Charlie, where you goin'?" Keefer called.

Payson did not answer, but then he answered Keefer

and Monroe only when it served his own purposes. They were handy for the time being, but he planned to drop them when he left Casper.

Though he had not let the two men have their entire share of money from the last holdup, he had given them enough to keep them quiet for a while. They were spending it all on liquor and women, but that was good. It kept them busy and out of his hair.

When Payson stepped up onto the board porch in front of the Crystal Palace, he heard piano music coming from inside. He noticed that it was the highbrow stuff that Smith often played. That was another thing Payson did not like about the piano player. Why didn't he just play the kind of music he was supposed to?

Inside the Crystal Palace, Amy had come down and was sitting at Angus's table, listening to the music. When Smith heard her gasp and saw her grow pale, he knew without having to ask that Fast Charlie Payson must have come into the saloon. He looked over at her and smiled reassuringly.

"Listen to this, Amy," he said. "This was a piece Liszt was working on. What do you think about it?" He moved quickly into the new number, and as he hoped it would, it had a calming effect on Amy.

Payson got his drink and then turned toward the piano. "Hey, piano player," he called.

Smith did not respond.

"Piano player, I'm talking to you!" Payson shouted, and again Amy involuntarily caught her breath. This time Smith stopped playing, and everyone in the saloon stopped talking. What had been a bright, cheerful place an instant before was now as quiet as a tomb.

"Oh, Smith," Amy whispered in fear, her words seeming to come to him from a distance, though she had now moved close to the piano.

Smith put his hand on hers to calm her, and then he turned on his bench, a cold smile on his face. "What do you want, albino?"

"I don't like to be called that," Payson said, flashing not only anger but surprise that anyone, especially a piano player, would have the nerve to call him that to his face.

"I'll try to remember," Smith said. "Now, perhaps you'll tell me why you interrupted my playing."

"That the only kind of music you know how to play? You've got no business playing in a bar if that's all you know. That's funeral music."

"I'm sure I have an adequate repertoire," Smith said. "But I prefer to play this kind of music, and none of the customers seems to mind."

"Yeah?" Payson took another swallow of his drink and then wiped the back of his hand across his tightly compressed pale lips. "Well, I'm a customer, and I mind."

"You're only one customer," Smith said. "And you're the only one who seems to mind."

"I'm the only one that counts. I want you to play 'Buffalo Gals,'" Payson said.

"I have a previous request from the lady. Now, if you'll excuse me," Smith said. He turned back to the piano.

"No," Payson said menacingly. "No, piano player, I'm not going to excuse you. You and I have something to settle, right here."

Smith turned around again and saw that Payson was holding his hand out at his right hip, just over the butt of his pistol.

"Like I said," Payson challenged, with an evil smile, "I want to hear 'Buffalo Gals.'"

Smith did not move.

"You heard me, piano player. Start playing."

"Why bother?" Smith asked. "You wouldn't know the difference whether I played it on a grand piano or on tin cans and baling wire."

"That doesn't matter. What matters is, you're going to play it."

"Very well. But before I play that kind of music, I have to have a drink. You don't mind?"

"Go ahead."

Smith walked to the bar and pointed to a bottle. "Fred,

you want to hand me my special blend?" he asked, matter-of-factly. Fred, who had moved to the other end of the bar when Payson began making his play, now started hesitantly toward the bottle. Smiling, Smith stopped him. "No, never mind," he said. "Our pale friend here has you so nervous I'm afraid you'll drop it, and it's the last bottle left. I'll get it myself." Smith walked around behind the bar and reached for the bottle. Then he held it out toward Payson. "Join me, Mr. Payson?"

"You aren't going to soft-soap me with a drink," Payson said. He pointed to the piano. "Now get back over there and play like I told you."

"I don't think I want to do that," Smith said. "I'm pretty particular about the people I play for."

"Damn your hide," Payson began, but he was interrupted by Amy.

"Oh, Smith, please," she pleaded. "Don't antagonize him."

"You better listen to your girlfriend, piano player," Payson said. "I'm not the kind of man you want to get mad."

"Well, now, you see, that's just the point. You're not a man," Smith said. "You're a maggot. You even look like one . . . white and slimy."

"What?" Payson screamed. "What did you call me?"

"I called you a maggot," Smith said quietly. There was a collective gasp from the crowd in the room, and at the same time sounds from the scraping and colliding of chairs as everyone hurried to get out of the line of fire.

"Get yourself a gun, piano player," Payson demanded, choked in fury. "Get yourself a gun, because I'm going to shoot you dead."

Smith smiled a cold, deadly smile that Payson recognized. It was the smile of a man who had faced death before and had won.

"Funny you'd say that," Smith went on, leaning forward with his hands just behind the bar. "Because I've got one. You see, Fred keeps a double-barreled shotgun back here, and I'm pointing it at you right now. If you so much as flinch, I'm going to pull both triggers. What's this thing loaded with, Fred?"

"D-double-aught buck," Fred answered nervously.

"Double-aught buck," Smith mused. "Let's see, I guess that would take out the front of the bar and about half of your insides. You'll die slowly, albino, flopping around like a gutted fish."

"If you've got a gun under that bar, bring it up and let me see it," Payson demanded, his feet moving itchily as he stood in the same spot.

"No, I don't think I want to do that," Smith said. "You see, while I'm bringing it up, you'll be drawing on me. No, I like it just the way it is. This way, if you make a move toward your gun, I can kill you."

"How do I know you even have a gun?"

"I guess you don't know," Smith said.

"You're a fool," Payson hissed.

"Well, now, how much of a fool can I be?" Smith asked. "I've got you covered, and I couldn't miss with this shotgun, even if I tried."

Payson licked his lips nervously, and his eyes narrowed as he stared at Smith.

"My advice to you, Mr. Payson," Smith went on calmly, "is for you to leave two bits on the counter to pay for your drink. Then get the hell out of here."

"Listen, friend," Payson hissed. "You better never let me see you walking around armed. If I do, you're dead. Understand?" He slapped the silver down on the counter and then angrily strode out.

For a long moment after the albino left, there was dead silence in the saloon. Then one of the men breathed a long sigh of relief and said, "Smith, I would've never thought it. You've got more guts than sense. Even standing there with a double-barreled shotgun in your hands, it took guts to call down the albino."

"I'll say," another said. "Damn if this don't call for a round of drinks. Set 'em up, Fred. I'm buyin'."

Fred was still at the opposite end of the bar, not having moved a muscle for the last minute. He continued to stare at Smith, his eyes wide open in shock.

"Come on, Fred, what's the matter with you?" the man questioned. "Didn't you hear what I said? Set 'em up for our brave friend here."

Without a word, Fred reached under the bar in front of him and pulled out the shotgun. He set the butt of it on the bar with the barrels pointing toward the ceiling.

"What the hell's that?" someone asked, at first not comprehending the significance of Fred's action.

"Oh, my God," Marybeth gasped. "Fred, are you telling me . . ."

"Smith didn't have no double-barreled shotgun, Miss Staley," Fred said. "I was standin' back here the whole time, just a-lookin' at him. He didn't have nothin' in his hand but a dishrag."

Angus, unaware of the drama that was being played out in the Crystal Palace, was standing in the office of the Coaltree Cross-country Express. Unlike the quiet ticket desk of his own office, the Coaltree desk was busy. Some of the customers purchasing the "two for one" tickets were people who had ridden many miles with Angus, and when they saw him there they looked away in embarrassment.

Angus did not blame them. DuMont had lowered his prices until it was impossible for him to compete anymore. Angus wished only that the people would understand that these prices could not possibly last. If he went out of business tomorrow, DuMont would immediately raise his prices higher than Angus's ever had been. Angus had talked to a couple of former customers about it, and they said they understood, but insisted that it would be foolish of them not to take advantage of the situation while they could.

Just outside the Coaltree office, Angus noticed the three thugs his employees had complained about. They were leaning against the front of the building, obviously not working. It was apparent that they had been hired for their brawling ability only.

"Well, Mr. Hightower," DuMont said, smiling broadly

when he saw Angus. "So you've come to give it up, have you? Well, that's a sensible move on your part."

"No, DuMont, I haven't," Angus said.

The smile left DuMont's face. "Then what do you want? I'm a busy man."

Angus pointed to the three bullyboys outside the office.

"I want to talk to you about those men," he said. "Do they work for you?"

"Yes. What about them?"

"What about them? Why, look at them, DuMont. Are they drivers? No. Do they tend to your stock? No. If you ask me, they're nothing but brawlers, and you hired them for just that reason."

To Angus's surprise, DuMont made no effort to disagree with him. "You're quite right, Mr. Hightower," he said. "They are brawlers, and I did hire them for just that reason."

Angus was taken aback. "You admit that?"

"Look at it my way, Mr. Hightower," DuMont went on. "I'm a businessman, not a fighter. But your men have been picking fights with my men."

"It hasn't all been one-sided," Angus said, but DuMont interrupted him with a wave of his hand.

"That doesn't matter. Now, if our competition is going to be trying to provide the best and fastest service at the lowest prices, then I'll compete with you in that way. But if there are going to be fights, then I have no choice but to hire men who are good fighters, and I'll compete with you in that way as well."

"I see," Angus said, surprised by DuMont's candor.

"I told you, Mr. Hightower, I plan to win this little competition we find ourselves in. You could save us both a lot of trouble and expense if you would just admit that you've lost. Then we could get on with serving the people of Casper with the best possible coach line."

"The people of Casper, huh?" Angus said. He turned and started to walk away, then stopped and looked back with an expression of disgust on his face. "You know, DuMont, if you hadn't said that, I might have been willing to listen to your proposition. But to say that you are concerned with the people of Casper? You hypocrite! You don't give a damn about the people of Casper or any other place. All you care about is running me out of business so you can look good to Ben Coaltree."

An oily grin appeared on DuMont's face.

"You may be right," he said. "But either way, Hightower, your days are numbered."

When Angus returned to the Crystal Palace, he was told that the piano player not only had faced Payson down but had accomplished the deed with a dishrag. The story was much too good to be contained inside the walls of the Crystal Palace, and by that night it had spread all over town. Everyone who supported Angus came into the Crystal Palace to celebrate, and soon the place took on the atmosphere of a party.

Amy was happy that Smith was not hurt, but she could not understand the attitude of those who wanted to celebrate the event. She was willing to concede that Smith had been courageous, perhaps even foolhardy, to stand up to Payson as he had. And considering the situation, he may have done the only reasonable thing. But if everyone celebrated it, Payson was bound to find out he had been played for a fool, and when he did find out, she feared he would come after Smith and kill him whether he was armed or not.

Unable to stay downstairs and watch what she considered to be dangerous activity, Amy went upstairs to her room. She lit the lantern by her bed, turning it down until the room was illuminated by a soft, golden bubble of light. Then she lay on her bed, listening to the noise from downstairs as she stared at the ceiling. She had been there for several minutes, when she heard a quiet knock on her door.

"Yes?" she called.

"Amy, it's me, Smith." She got up and went to the door. When she opened it, she saw him standing in the shadows of the hallway. "Are you all right?" he asked.

"Yes, of course I'm all right. Why would you ask?"

"You came upstairs without so much as a word," Smith said.

"I . . . I didn't like what was going on."

"You mean everyone celebrating the fact that I fooled Payson?"

"You didn't just fool Payson. You made a fool of him," Amy said. "There's a huge difference, and I'm afraid for you. I wish they would all just go home."

"Amy, Payson has been running over the people of this town long enough," Smith said. "They needed some sort of victory, something to show them that he isn't invincible."

"Why did you have to be the one to give it to them?" Amy asked. "You're a musician, not a gunfighter."

Smith smiled. "That's nice," he said.

"What's nice?" she asked in an exasperated tone of voice.

"That you're concerned for me," he said. He reached up and touched her lightly on the cheek. She was amazed by the feel of his fingers, cool as ice at the point of contact, yet possessed of some magical means of suffusing her entire body with heat.

"Of course I'm concerned for you," Amy said, trying to ignore what the touch of his fingers was doing to her.

"I love the way your lips shine in this light," Smith said. "The way your hair falls to your shoulders in a soft cloud. I love the way your brows arch so charmingly over your eyes, and the way those eyes leap out to grab my heart and hold it captive with their beauty."

Amy knew she must be blushing furiously. No man had ever spoken to her in such a manner, and she found his words, spoken with his soft, southern drawl, utterly charming and exciting. And yet, she felt she should stop him. She should not stand here in the doorway of her room and listen to a man speak so boldly to her. It was just not proper!

"Don't," she said in a whisper. "Please, Smith, don't speak to me in this way."

"All right," he said with a serious face. He looked at her

without speaking, holding her gaze so long and with such intensity that Amy became nervous.

"And you shouldn't look at me like that, either," she said.

Smith sighed softly. "Well, it seems I can't talk to you, and I can't look at you. I guess that leaves only one thing."

"What?"

"This," he said in a tender voice.

Before she realized what was going on, Smith turned her chin up with one finger and bent down to kiss her lips. The kiss, totally unexpected, took away her consciousness of time and place and circumstances, and she found herself responding to it, kissing him in return with fully as much ardor.

Once, when Amy had been a little girl, she had fallen from a tree, and the breath had been knocked from her body. It had been a strange, frightening, reeling sensation, lying there not knowing quite what had happened or where she was, or if she would ever breathe again. And now his kiss brought the same sensation flooding through her.

Finally, he pulled away from her. He looked at her for a long, tender moment, and then he smiled at her in an awkward, whimsical way.

"Good night, my sweet Amy," he said. He turned and walked down the hall toward his own room, while Amy, still afire with sensation, returned to her bed. She extinguished the lantern and then lay there breathing in the dark, the kiss from Smith still a real presence on her lips.

So this is it, she thought. *This is what it's like to be in love.*

Chapter Ten

The stagecoach wheel rims were covered with steel bands, which rolled over the hard dirt road with a muffled crunching sound. As the wheels whirled around, dirt adhered to the rims for about half a revolution before being thrown back in little rooster tails. Over the mountains hung the midafternoon sun, and far away down in the valley the hot air kicked up dust devils that skipped out randomly across the prairie.

Deekus rode high on the driver's seat, looking out over the broad backs of the six horses, loving this land and all it represented. Some people said the time would come when stagecoaches would no longer be used, and trains would connect every town and city in America. But Deekus knew that it would be far enough in the future not to affect him. He was sure there would be coaches to drive for as long as he wanted to drive them.

As much as he loved driving a coach, however, he had already made up his mind that he would not drive for Coaltree Cross-country Express. No, sir, not even if they doubled what Angus Hightower was paying him. If Angus was run out of business, Deekus figured he would just have to find another line of work, even if it meant working in the stable.

Deekus recalled Crack Kendall's remark about shoveling horse manure in the stables. If it came to that, by God he would be willing to do it. He remembered, also, the

satisfaction he had felt when his doubled-up fist had connected with Crack's nose, and he chuckled.

"What's so funny?" Blakely asked. Blakely, who was
riding shotgun on the seat beside Deekus, shifted his
position slightly and pulled out a twist of tobacco. He
offered a chew to Deekus, but Deekus refused. Blakely
was in his late twenties, a small, wiry man who had
knocked about from job to job. For the last six months he
had worked for Angus in whatever capacity Angus wanted.
He had been one of the men in the big fight at the Angry
Bull and, like Deekus, had gone to jail for it.

"I was thinkin' about Crack," Deekus said. "And how
he's gonna look when his nose heals."

Blakely cut off a plug of tobacco, stuck it in his mouth,
and then chewed thoughtfully for a moment.

"Ugly as he is, don't reckon it's gonna make a whole lot
of difference," he said. "I always thought Crack was a
pretty good man. I just can't see him workin' for DuMont."

"I guess he's gotta make a livin' just like the rest of us,"
Deekus said.

Blakely spit over the edge of the rolling wheel. "Reckon
you're right," he agreed.

Blakely was making this trip as a shotgun guard because
they had expected to transfer one thousand dollars from
the Bank of Medicine Bow to the Carbon County Bank in
Casper. When they went to the Bank of Medicine Bow,
however, the money was not ready, and they learned that
the transaction would not take place until the next day. As
it turned out, there were no passengers either, so the trip
need not have been made at all, except to satisfy the
Wyoming Rapid Express commitment to make two runs
per day. They had picked up a couple of letters, and the
Medicine Bow office of Rapid Express did put forty dollars
in the strongbox to take back to Casper. But even that
could have been handled by the next stage.

It was such a quiet trip back that when three riders with
guns drawn suddenly blocked the road in front of the
stage, their unexpected appearance startled the driver and
guard as much as it spooked the horses. The front two

animals balked and reared, and Deekus had to fight the contorted ribbons of the reins to bring his team under control. Had there been any passengers in the coach, they would have been roughly thrown about by the sudden twisting stop.

All three riders wore long dusters and hoods.

"Mister, you done made a big mistake," Deekus called out to the man riding ahead of the other two. "We ain't carryin' no money."

"I'd like to just take a look-see myself if you don't mind. Open the strong box," the rider called back to him.

"What do you want me to do?" Blakely asked.

"Open the box for Mr. Payson," Deekus said. "Let him look for himself."

"Hold it with that strongbox, mister," the bandit said. He turned his attention back to Deekus. "You think you're pretty smart, huh? You think you know who I am?"

"I don't have to be all that smart to know who you are," Deekus challenged. "What I don't understand is why you're even botherin' to wear a hood. You already know that if I tell the sheriff, he ain't gonna do nothin' about it."

"That's right. You just remember that, and everything will work out just fine," the robber said.

"The only thing is, I just wish I had me a dishrag so I could set you to runnin'," Deekus answered.

"What did you say?" the leader of the bandits asked in an angry, choked voice.

"You heard me," Deekus replied. "I was there the other night when the piano player run you off with no more in his hands than a dishrag."

"You thought that was funny, did you?"

"I enjoyed it," Deekus admitted.

The man pulled the duster back to expose his holster and then slipped his pistol into it. He pointed to Blakely. "Give the driver your gun," he said, spitting out the words as if they were hot coals.

"Hey, what are you doing?" one of the other bandits asked.

"I'm going to show the loudmouth, here, that I'm not afraid to go up against a shotgun."

"You're crazy! You don't have to take no chance like that. Let's get the money and get out of here."

"Don't worry. I'll be taking the chance, not you. If he kills me, you kill him."

"Give me the gun," Deekus said to Blakely, reaching for it.

"Deekus, they got you in a corner. No matter what you do, they're gonna kill you," Blakely told him.

"I know that, but give it to me anyway," Deekus said, taking the shotgun. Deekus looked at the leader and smiled. It was a cold smile, icy with the chill of anger and fear. "I'm thinkin' it just might be worth it."

"That's what I'm wanting you to think, old man. Now point the gun at me. Whenever you're ready, pull the trigger."

"Deekus, no!" Blakely said.

"Lean back outta the way, Blakely," Deekus said. "I'm gonna kill this son of a bitch no matter what those other two galoots do."

Deekus looked down at the shotgun in his hands and then at the hooded rider in front of him. He remembered young Billy Sinclair and the sense of outrage he had felt when he had learned of the boy's death. That same sense of anger flooded through him again. He stood up and pulled back the hammers of the shotgun, but that was as far as he got. The pistol suddenly appeared in the robber's hand as if by magic. With the same motion that brought the gun to his hand, the robber fired. It all happened in a split second, after Deekus began to cock the two shotgun hammers and before he could pull a trigger.

As if detached from his own body, Deekus watched events unfold with calm certainty and an acceptance of his own death. He saw the muzzle flash and then felt the .44 caliber bullet embed itself in his chest. He was not aware of any pain, just a burning weight in his chest, a weight so heavy that he could not stand up to it. The impact knocked him back against the top of the coach. He dropped the shotgun and reached out to grab the rail, missed, and then tumbled over the side and fell to the ground. He landed faceup, his arms flung out beside him on the dirt, the unfired shotgun still on the driver's box.

"Deekus!" Blakely called to him.

Deekus heard the voice, but it was faint and far away, as if it were coming from the bottom of a deep, deep barrel. He felt warm and comfortable, and he closed his eyes, knowing he would never open them again.

"Don't waste your breath. You're talkin' to a dead man," the robber said. "Now open that money box like I said."

"Jesus, mister, we told you the truth. We ain't carryin' nothin'. There ain't but forty dollars in this box," the guard said. "You killed Deekus for forty dollars!"

"Forty dollars or forty thousand, it doesn't make any difference," the robber answered. "I plan to take every penny this stage line carries until you quit business."

Angus stood in the back room of the undertaker's parlor, looking at the nude body of his driver. He felt a lump in his throat and a burning sensation in his eyes.

Deekus had not been a very big man in life, and in death he seemed even smaller. His chest was narrow, and Angus could plainly see the outline of his ribs under the white skin. The bullet hole was black and ugly. Both eyes were closed, and the expression on his face was almost a smile, as if Deekus were enjoying some joke from the other side.

"Good-bye, old friend," Angus said quietly, his voice catching on the words.

"I'll take care of everything, Mr. Hightower," the undertaker promised.

"Fine, fine. Send me the bill," Angus said. The least he could do was provide a first-class funeral for a man who had died in his service.

When Angus returned to the Crystal Palace, he found Blakely waiting for him, as Angus had requested. Blakely was sitting with Marybeth, drinking a beer. White foam from the beer hung in the guard's mustache.

"Did you see him?" Blakely asked as Angus joined them at the table.

"Yes, I saw him."

"He must'a been hit right in the heart. He died quick," Blakely said.

"What was it you said Payson told you?"

Blakely was taking a drink of beer as Angus asked his question. He brought the mug down quickly and then shook his head. His eyes were wide with fear.

"I didn't say it was Payson," he said. "He was wearing a hood . . . they was all wearin' hoods. How could I see who he was, if he was wearin' a hood?"

"Whoever it was, he put on a show for you with his quick draw, didn't he?"

"Yes, sir, he done that, all right. I never seen nothin' like it in my whole life. He put his gun in his holster an' told Deekus to shoot anytime he wanted. But Deekus only got the hammers back, and before he could fire, the robber had his gun out and blazin'."

"But you don't think it was Payson."

"I didn't say that," Blakely said. "What I said was, I wasn't going to *say* it was Payson."

"All right, all right. It doesn't matter," Angus said. "Right now, I'm more interested in what the robber said when you told him you were only carrying forty dollars."

"He said it didn't make no difference how much money we was carryin'. He said he planned to take every penny until the stage line quit."

"That sounds almost as if running me out of business is more important than the amount of money the robberies take in," Angus said.

"Angus, you're not saying DuMont had anything to do with it, are you?" Marybeth asked.

"No, I'm not ready to say that yet," Angus said. "Even though DuMont has the most to gain by that happening, I don't think even he would go that far. But it is an interesting turn of events, don't you think?"

"I would say it's more frightening than interesting," Marybeth insisted. "Look, maybe DuMont does have a good idea about sending some of the money shipments with his stagecoaches. Why don't you do that—let him get held up once in a while?"

"I may have to resort to that," Angus said. "But if I do, it's the beginning of the end, because it's the same as admitting to my shippers that I can't get their money through."

"I wish there were some way you could just sneak the money back and forth," Marybeth mused.

Angus looked at Marybeth and smiled, and then he snapped his fingers. "Marybeth, I believe you've just hit upon the answer."

"What do you mean?"

"I know how I'm going to get the money through. Whenever there's a shipment, I'll make a secret run during the middle of the night. One coach will leave from Casper and the other from Medicine Bow. They'll meet halfway between the two towns, transfer the money from one coach to the other, then return to their starting points in time to make the morning runs."

"Angus, your drivers won't get any rest," Marybeth said.

"I've got to hire a new driver to replace Deekus anyway. Blakely, do you want to drive for me, instead of guard?"

"Sure, Mr. Hightower. Whatever you want, I'll do," Blakely said.

"All right, you'll take Deekus's place. I'll hire an extra driver, and I'll also drive, so we can handle the work."

"I have just one question," Marybeth said.

"What?"

"How long do you think you can keep up with such a schedule?" Marybeth asked.

"As long as it takes," Angus answered resolutely.

Percy Rawlings, seated at his desk in the San Francisco headquarters of Coaltree Cross-country Express Company, began to reread the letter he had just received from his employer. He had worked for the company long enough to know that what might be considered a strange request for anyone else could be a normal course of action for Ben

Coaltree. Mr. Coaltree wanted his finest private coach and six perfectly matched horses loaded on a train and shipped to Medicine Bow, Wyoming. What's more, Mr. Coaltree wanted Percy to accompany the coach. In Medicine Bow, Percy would meet Ben Coaltree. Then Percy would take him to Casper.

Percy was relieved to learn that Ben Coaltree would be personally attending to the company's affairs in Casper soon. There was another employee, Wesley DuMont, about whom Percy was concerned. Recently, DuMont had been overstepping his role in the company's affairs, requesting unusually large sums of money for expenses and giving himself the title of Ben Coaltree's executive secretary— none of which Percy had let slip by him. Rather than taking the young man to task himself, however, Percy had seen the opportunity for Coaltree and DuMont both to be in Casper during Amy Coaltree's visit, and he had written to his employer, suggesting that he look into the situation himself. Percy was honored to learn that Coaltree wanted him present as well.

It would be good, Percy thought, to see Mr. Coaltree again. Though Percy was the only one in the entire organization who ever saw Coaltree at all, even he saw him only rarely, for Ben Coaltree was a genuine recluse.

Once a lion of San Francisco society, Coaltree had long ago dropped out of sight, withdrawing from all the clubs and organizations he had so ardently supported. He saw fewer and fewer people, took less and less interest in his business, and stayed for days at a time in his room, sometimes without even getting dressed.

Despite his personal inattention, his far-flung business empire continued to flourish. Ben Coaltree had established a business operation that was self-sustaining. Along with a top-notch staff, there were bankers, managers, and accountants at the various levels to make all the decisions necessary to keep Coaltree Cross-country Express one of the most profitable firms in America.

Percy Rawlings was the best example of the high-quality staff Coaltree had working for him. Percy's position was just under Coaltree, and top executives from all over the country dealt directly with him. Only Percy knew where to contact Coaltree at any given moment. As a result, Percy had a great deal of power, and many decisions that people thought were coming from Coaltree were in fact coming from Percy Rawlings. It was a tribute to Percy's loyalty to Ben Coaltree that he had never abused his position. When he made an independent decision, he made the one he truly thought would be most in keeping with Coaltree's wishes.

Percy remembered the letter from Coaltree's daughter and remembered sending her money and railroad tickets, so he was not at all surprised that Coaltree was making plans to see her. He wondered about Amy Coaltree and what she was like now. He had been present the night she was born, and had shared Ben Coaltree's joy over being a father. He remembered standing in the library of the Coaltree mansion, having a brandy to celebrate, and being shocked when Coaltree disclosed to him his wife's unhappiness with the West. Coaltree had loved her dearly and had surrounded her with every luxury—oil paintings and statuary by European masters, porcelain from the Ming dynasty of China, carpets from the looms of Persia, and furniture made by the finest craftsmen in England. But Amy's mother had not been satisfied and had vowed not to raise their daughter in a place she considered wild and uncivilized.

It was after his wife left him, taking the baby, that Ben Coaltree had begun to change. He had withdrawn more and more into himself, seeing no one but Percy and communicating with no one in his business except through Percy. Coaltree had begun going out of his way to avoid the life of the privileged classes, preserving his anonymity while he pursued a life of outdoor work and adventure. Then he had acquired the habit of taking long trips, traveling in disguise under an assumed name, sometimes as a passenger on his own coach line. He faced the hardships of long stage trips with his fellow passengers, who never knew that the large, friendly man with them was, in fact, one of the wealthiest men in America.

Percy recalled seeing him once dressed in deerskin clothing, with a long scraggly beard. Coaltree had just returned home from spending the winter in the mountains with two other prospectors, looking for gold. He had done it not for the opportunity to increase his fortune, but rather for the joy of looking. The unique thing about it was that Percy knew that Coaltree—who had called himself John Witherspoon during this period—had faced the same dangers and hardships as his partners in the expedition, and had almost lost his life braving a winter blizzard to rescue one of them from the top of a mountain.

For a time he worked as a buffalo hunter for the Union Pacific railroad, and even though his buffalo-hunting job granted him a free pass for the first-class section on any train, he had told Percy he always chose to ride in an immigrant car at the sooty tail end of the train. Ironically, often at the front of the same train was a private car belonging to Coaltree Cross-country Express and used by its executives, but he never availed himself of the amenities he had won by the sweat of his brow.

Coaltree was well aware of the authority and responsibilities his absences gave to Percy Rawlings, but over the years Coaltree had learned that his confidence in his right-hand man was well placed.

Percy at this moment was hurrying to the railroad station to make the arrangements for shipping the coach and horses Mr. Coaltree had requested. He was glad that his employer was going to meet his daughter in style. That, finally, was as it should be.

"This is the second night in a row that Hightower's stage has gone out just after dark and come back just before mornin'," Blair Morann told DuMont.

DuMont walked over to the front door of his office and looked outside. Although it was dark, the moon shone brightly above the town, and several of the brightly lighted saloons spilled patches of glowing yellow onto the street.

He could hear pianos playing different tunes, and from

one of the saloons came a man's loud guffaw, followed by the high-pitched trill of a woman's laughter. He turned to look back at Morann.

"I don't know what they're doing, running at night," he said. "Maybe he's experimenting with some way to improve his schedule. Was he carrying passengers tonight?"

"No."

"Who was driving?"

"Why, Angus was driving hisself," Morann said.

"Hmmm. That's interesting. Maybe I'll wander over to the Crystal Palace and see if I can find out anything."

Amy saw DuMont as he came into the saloon. For a moment she thought about going up to her room to avoid him, but she had promised Marybeth she would stay downstairs for a while. So when DuMont started toward her, she had no recourse but to be as pleasant as she could.

"Good evening, Amy," DuMont said.

"Mr. DuMont," Amy replied. Though her voice was not angry, it was cool.

"I, uh, came over here to apologize to Mr. Smith," DuMont said.

Amy brightened a little. "Really?"

"Yes. And to you. I was wrong to pick a fight with him the other night. And I was wrong to assume that our relationship was anything beyond seeing you safely to Casper. Will you forgive me?"

"I . . . I suppose so," Amy said, hoping that this signaled a turnaround in the conflicts besetting the town.

"And Mr. Smith?"

"You'll have to ask him," Amy said. "He's going to join me as soon as he finishes this number. You can talk to him then."

"What does he like to drink? I'll buy drinks all around the table."

"Ask Fred," Amy said. "Smith has a special blend he likes."

DuMont went to the bar just as Marybeth returned to the table. She nodded toward DuMont, asking Amy, "What does he want?"

"He wants to buy us drinks and apologize," Amy said.

Marybeth smiled and sat down. "Good. While he's at it, perhaps he'll tell us that he's decided to pull out and leave Angus alone."

DuMont did apologize, and he was polished enough to make it sound sincere. He did not offer to pull out of Casper, though. What he did was try to pump the three of them for information. It soon became evident to all of them that he was dying to find out why Angus was making unscheduled night runs with his coaches. When he left a half hour later without any more knowledge than he had when he came in, Amy, Marybeth, and Smith laughed.

"Don't you love seeing him scratch around for information, like the neighborhood gossip at the back fence?" Marybeth asked.

Smith held up his glass. "Ladies, I propose a toast."

When the others held their glasses up to his, he smiled.

"Here is to Wes DuMont," he said. "May his senses be confounded and his confusion grow, and may he always be a day late and a dollar short."

Chapter Eleven

Crack Kendall had noticed that morning on the trip back from Medicine Bow that one of the horses seemed to be favoring a shoulder. Unharnessing the team, Crack saw that the animal was chafed, so he applied liniment to the sore and then began working on the harness to ensure a better fit. In a far corner of the stable, a small section occupied by Wyoming Rapid Express horses, Peters and Winfield, two of Hightower's men, were cleaning stalls. Seeing Crack Kendall at work, the two men walked toward him.

"Hey, Crack, how's your nose?" Peters called, as they approached.

Crack and Peters had been friends before the intense competition between the two stage lines put them in opposite camps. They had hunted together, had gotten drunk and chased women together, and had worked side by side. It was just a matter of circumstances that put them in opposing positions now.

Peters punctuated his question by handing Crack a bottle. Crack smiled at the offer of friendship and took a long swallow of whiskey before handing back the bottle.

"I'll tell you this," Crack said. "I can whistle pert' near any song you want with my mouth closed. All I got to do is breathe."

All three men laughed.

"Deekus done that to you, did he? I didn't know that wiry little bastard had it in him," Winfield said.

"Neither did I," Crack admitted, touching his nose gingerly with a forefinger.

Peters took a drink and then said somberly, "I'm goin' to miss ol' Deekus. He was a good man to have around in a pinch."

"Yeah," Crack said. "I wish they'd catch whoever's doin' all the robbin'. None of our coaches have been robbed yet, but I don't mind tellin' you, I keep a sharp lookout every time I go out."

"Here comes somebody," Peters interjected. "You better get back to whatever you was doin'. It wouldn't look good for us to be jawin', bein' as we're supposed to be workin' against one another."

"That's somethin' else I wish," Crack said as he picked up the harness again. "I wish these highfalutin' bosses would get things straightened out between 'em so us workin' men could get on with each other like decent folks should."

"Ain't that the truth?" Winfield said, echoing the sentiments.

Crack looked up to see who was coming into the stable and saw the three men DuMont had most recently hired. Crack did not like them, so he had made no effort to learn their names, and he decided to ignore them now. They did no work whatever—all they did was brawl—but they drew as much money as anyone on the payroll. While everyone else was working, these three men sat around in the shade or played cards in one of the saloons.

There were still a few fights in the saloons at night, but not very many. The fight in which Deekus had broken Crack's nose had been mainly the result of high spirits and too much liquor; as far as barroom brawls went, it had almost been fun. But the fights had become nasty and brutal, and they were instigated by the three galoots who had just entered the stable. Since the fighting had turned serious, most of the regular workingmen of the Coaltree and Hightower operations were avoiding situations where fights might break out, especially in the saloons. That was frustrating for the three men, since they now had to go to great lengths to get a fight started.

With the harness reworked, Crack wanted to see how it would fit on the sore horse, but the animal had wandered out into the pen. Crack walked outside to find it. Five minutes later, when he had come back into the barn from the bright sunlight and his eyes had adjusted, he noticed, with some degree of relief, that the three thugs were gone.

He called out, "Peters, Winfield, them galoots gone?"

"Crack? Crack, help us." The voice was thin and pained.

"Peters?" Crack called out, and moved quickly over to the Hightower stalls. He gave an involuntary groan when he saw Peters and Winfield lying on the dirt floor. Both men had been badly beaten; their faces were bruised, swollen, and covered with blood. To add insult to injury, all the manure the men had cleaned from the stalls had been dumped on them.

"Just stay quiet!" Crack said, turning immediately to leave. "I'll get the doc!"

Big Troy picked up the piece of metal from the forge with long tongs and held it on the anvil. The narrow strip of iron was glowing red, and as Big Troy hammered it, showers of sparks erupted at each blow. Behind him on blocks sat one of Angus Hightower's stages, the front axle removed so Big Troy could repair the tie bar. Angus was in Medicine Bow and probably did not even know about the damaged tie bar, but Blakely had brought it in just after completing his run, and Big Troy had promised to have it out by tonight.

"Hey, you, nigger. I need you to shoe a horse for me."

Big Troy turned toward the voice and saw three men standing just inside the door of his shop. He did not know them by name, but he and everyone else knew who they were. Since they had come to town three days ago, they had sent at least five men to the doctor. Though none of them was as big as Troy himself, or John Meeker, all three were large, powerful men, and they were supremely confident in their ability to intimidate others.

"You gennel'men are standin' in my light," Big Troy said.

"Oh, now, is that a fact? Did you hear the nigger? We're standin' in his light."

"I believe it. Look, it's so dark in there he's done disappeared. Hey, nigger, where are you?"

Big Troy seethed inside, but right this minute the task before him was more important than his pride. He had promised Blakely he would have the tie bar done before nightfall, and he intended to do just that. He put the piece of metal back in the forge and then pumped the bellows until the fire was blazing. The tie bar began to glow again.

"Hey, nigger, when white folks are talkin' to you, it ain't polite to pay them no never mind. I told you, I got a horse I need shoed."

"I'll get to your horse soon as I can. Right now, I'se tied up with this stage." Big Troy pulled the glowing metal from the fire again.

"What? You mean *this* stage? Why, suppose we just take care of it for you?"

The one who was talking picked up a sledgehammer and started splintering the spokes out of the wheels. He was joined by the other two, and they laughed as if breaking up the stage were a carnival competition.

At first Big Troy was shocked that they would be so wantonly destructive; then he boiled over with rage. With a roar like an angry bull he rushed toward them, still holding the tie bar, glowing cherry red, in the tongs. He pushed the hot iron against the shoulders of the ringleader, and the thug let out a bellow of pain that could be heard all up and down the street.

"Curly! The nigger!" one of the others warned, but he was the one in more immediate danger. Dropping the tie bar and tongs, Big Troy turned and smashed a fist into his face, shattering several teeth, and the bully went down with blood streaming from his mouth. Next Big Troy swung at the one called Curly, but Curly, forewarned, managed to pull his head aside just in time. Big Troy's right fist sailed by Curly's head and crashed through the door of the stage. Big Troy pulled it out, tearing away half the door panel as he did so.

By now the leader of the group, the one Big Troy had burned with the tie bar, had recovered enough to join in the fray. He raised the sledgehammer over his head, intending to smash Big Troy with it. Big Troy sent a whistling left to the hammer wielder's face, and the man dropped the sledge behind him and sagged at the knees.

Big Troy's initial roar and the ringleader's bellow of pain had attracted the attention of several townsmen, and by now they and others were gathered in front of the blacksmith's shop. They stood in the street and watched the four men inside fighting it out, three against one. It was soon apparent that the odds meant nothing, because one by one DuMont's thugs went down under Big Troy's hammering blows, and when they managed to get up, they were knocked back down even more decisively. Less than five minutes after the fight started, all three of DuMont's men were lying unconscious in the dirt—more badly beaten than Peters and Winfield had been.

The Crystal Palace was unusually busy that afternoon, because the Rapid Express employees were celebrating Big Troy's whipping of DuMont's three thugs. Chief among the celebrants were Peters and Winfield. The two men were cleaned up now, and they had been treated by the doctor, but their faces were swollen and black and blue from their earlier encounter. Crack came in with them, assisting Peters, who could barely walk, even with help. A few men started in on Crack with jibes, but he stopped them in their tracks by announcing that he had quit DuMont.

"I won't work for a man who hires people to beat up workin' men for no good reason," Crack said.

"Why, Crack, you was right in the middle of things the other night," someone reminded him.

"Yes, sir, I reckon I was at that. But that was a fair fight amongst the workers. There weren't no barroom brawlers brought in just to be breakin' heads."

"Well, them barroom brawlers met their match when they run up against Big Troy," Winfield said, smiling through split lips. "Fred, give Big Troy whatever he wants to drink."

Though he was being treated as a special guest that day, Big Troy was always welcome in the Crystal Palace. He reminded Marybeth a great deal of Sam, the giant overseer on her father's plantation back in Mississippi. It was not just because he was big or black, but because there was a nobility about him, a goodness of character, that was apparent to all who looked for it.

Big Troy often came to the Crystal Palace to see Angus there on business, but the blacksmith rarely visited the saloon for pleasure. This afternoon, however, he was standing at the head of the bar, the uncomfortable recipient of the town's accolades. He was not accustomed to drinking until later in the day, but his seeming unease was caused not only by that irregularity; he was also thinking of the unfinished work in his shop, while trying very hard to disregard the pain in his right hand.

"I s'pose I could drink another beer," he said, and Fred drew one from the tap and slid it down the bar to him.

A few more men came into the saloon, laughing and talking about what was going on over at the Angry Bull.

"You should see 'em," they said. "All the Coaltree guys are over there cryin' in their beer, and the three men that Big Troy beat up? Why, they're all bandaged up, sittin' in the corner as calm as mewin' little kittens."

"Yeah, we told 'em to send out anybody they want. Ole Troy can whip 'em one at a time or all together. It don't make no never mind to Big Troy. Hey, Fred! Give Big Troy another drink, why don't you?" Fred drew another beer and slid it down to Big Troy, who nodded politely and thanked the men for buying it.

Because of all the talk, no one was in the mood for listening to piano music, so Smith was sitting at the table next to the piano with Marybeth and Amy. Angus had gone to Medicine Bow, not to return until the next day.

"Poor Troy," Marybeth said. "I'm afraid they're going to draw him into a fight with Meeker, whether he wants in or not."

"Most fights are like that," Smith observed. "It seems the people who least want them are the ones who are doing the fighting. The others sort of goad them on."

"Maybe Big Troy will find a way to avoid it," Amy proposed.

"No," Smith said. "Big Troy knows it's coming, and he's ready for it."

The object of their speculation finished his beer at the bar and then walked over to the table and looked at Smith. Smith had often studied the eyes of men under pressure, and looking into Big Troy's eyes, he saw an acceptance of things as they were, and a determination to make the best of it.

"Mista Smith, you recollect I told you one day I would have to fight Mista Meeker?"

"Yes."

"I reckon that day soon be comin'," he said.

"Big Troy, you can handle him," Smith said.

Big Troy smiled. "Yes, sir, I reckon I can." He rubbed his right fist with his left, and Smith thought he saw a slight wince. "I reckon I can," the big man said again. He turned then and walked out the door alone, looking back once with a smile and nod to acknowledge the shouts and cheers of everyone in the saloon.

Just as Big Troy went out the door, the telegrapher came in. He saw Amy, came over, and handed her a telegram.

"This just come for you, Miss Coaltree," he said.

"Why, thank you," Amy replied. She read the telegram and then smiled broadly. "At last!" she said.

"What is it?"

"My father! He's in Medicine Bow. He'll be here tomorrow."

"Well," Marybeth said with a big smile of her own. "We finally get to meet the mysterious Ben Coaltree."

"Oh, I wish Angus were here, though," Amy said. "I want him to meet my father."

"He'll be here. He promised me he would be back on the morning stage," Marybeth said.

"I, uh, think I'll go up to my room," Smith said.

"What? Oh, no! Why?" Amy asked.

"I think it's best," Smith answered. He pushed the chair back and walked away without another word. Amy looked toward him and then back at Marybeth. Her eyes showed her confusion.

"Marybeth, what is it?" she asked. "Why did he just walk away like that? What's wrong?"

Marybeth put her hand across the table to touch the younger woman's hand. "Don't you understand, dear? Your father is one of the wealthiest men in America. Smith is a piano player in a saloon. In spite of the way Smith feels about you, I think he feels inadequate to meet your father because of the distance between them."

"But I love him," Amy said. Then she quickly covered her lips with both hands. It was the first time she had ever expressed aloud her feelings toward Smith.

"Do you?" Marybeth asked.

"Yes," Amy said after a moment. "I don't care if he is a saloon piano player or if he cleans the stables for Angus. I love him."

"Then go to him," Marybeth urged. "Go to him and tell him you love him."

Amy smiled and then stood up. "I will," she said. "I will go to him, and I'll tell him just how I feel."

When Amy reached Smith's room a moment later, the door was standing ajar. She pushed it open quietly and saw the man she loved standing at the window, looking out onto the street. His back was to the door, so he did not see her as she stepped into the room. Not until he heard her shut the door behind her did he know she was there.

At the sound, he turned toward her. "You shouldn't be here."

"Why not?"

"Because we have no chance, you and I. We are—"

"In love."

"What?"

"We are in love," Amy repeated. She walked over and put her hand on his chest. "Oh, Smith, you can't deny it, can you? I'm not an experienced woman, but I am possessed of some intelligence, and I know I'm not wrong when I read it in your eyes. You love me, Smith. You love me every bit as much as I love you. I see it every time you look at me, I hear it every time you speak my name. I know it when you play for me. I can't be that wrong, can I? You do love me, don't you?"

Smith was silent for a long moment, and Amy experienced a sense of great apprehension. Had she made a mistake?

"You're right," he finally said, though the words caught in his throat. "I love you," he said, clearly and loudly this time, but his voice wavered. He put his arms around her then, pulled her to him, and pressed his lips against hers.

A tide of exciting sensations swept over Amy. But she also felt bewildered and somehow frightened. He had kissed her before, and she had experienced the same quick flash of heat. But the other times had been spontaneous and unexpected, and more limited by circumstances. Now they were alone, in his room, and she could feel danger. She knew fear, yes, but more than fear she knew desire, desire that grew with each passing second.

Smith kissed her with sensuous lips. His lips traveled downward from her mouth, and she surrendered her neck to his caresses, allowing him to do what he wished, bending like a slender reed in a strong spring breeze. If it was his desire, she would gladly allow him to possess her fully, and she would . . .

But Smith found the strength Amy lacked, and he broke off the kiss, not abruptly, but tenderly, and then held her to him and stroked her hair.

"Amy, I couldn't give you the kind of life your father would want for you," he said.

"Don't you think my father would want me to be happy?"

"Yes, I suppose."

"You can give me happiness, my darling. All I need is for you to love me."

Smith smiled. "If that's all it takes, Amy, then I guess I can make you happy."

Ben Coaltree was staying in the Royal Suite of the Morning Star Hotel in Medicine Bow. The Royal Suite was so named because a Russian count had once stayed there during a hunting trip to America. Now it was reserved for the most special guests, the occasional traveling railroad dignitary, a visiting U.S. senator or cabinet officer, or a member of America's own royalty—the princes of power in business.

As soon as Percy Rawlings had arrived in Medicine Bow, he had arranged for the suite to be held for Ben Coaltree. Meanwhile, the special coach and team had been off-loaded and taken to the hotel's private stable. Tonight Percy had ordered dinner to be served for his employer and himself in their private dining room, and now he and Coaltree were sitting down to their evening meal.

Ben Coaltree was wearing a jacket of dark green velvet, chocolate brown trousers, a yellow silk vest, and a white, ruffled shirt topped by a green ascot. He looked as natural in the elegant dress as if he had been wearing such clothes every day without a break, though Percy knew that was not the case. He was not exactly sure where Coaltree had been or what he had been doing for the last six months, but judging from previous episodes, Percy was sure that Coaltree had spent the time in a way that was out of the ordinary. He knew Coaltree had received the weekly mail pouches, but beyond that, Percy had remained discreet and had not asked uninvited questions.

"I apologize for the accommodations," Percy said. "I'm afraid it was the best I could do in this place."

Coaltree looked around the dining room. The chandelier bathed the chamber in a resplendent golden light,

with each of its hundreds of glass facets sparkling like
diamonds. The furnishings of the room were in deep blue
velvet, and the carpet a rich, red wine color. The table
was covered with a beautiful damask cloth and laid with
china, silver, and crystal, all of which glistened in the soft
light.

"I've ordered Beef Wellington," Percy went on. "I hope
it's to your liking."

"Percy, will you for God's sake quit treating me like the
king of Prussia?" Coaltree demanded. "You know how I've
been living for the last twenty-two years."

"Well, not exactly," Percy admitted. "Though I have
had occasional glimpses."

"Yes, well, I haven't been wearing silk vests and eating
Beef Wellington, I can tell you that." He cleared his
throat, making a grumble of discontent. "But I'll tell you
this. I've enjoyed life a hell of a lot more than if I had
been living like a . . . a peacock."

"Yes, sir. I'm sorry if I've offended you."

Coaltree waved his hand. "Don't be ridiculous. I know
you've become accustomed to this life-style, and I don't
begrudge it. You've earned it by keeping control of things
and allowing me to live my life as I see fit. Besides, I
know you too well to be offended by you."

"Thank you, sir."

Coaltree took a bite of the Beef Wellington and then
smiled. "And I must admit, this beats the hell out of beans
and bacon."

"I'm glad you approve, sir."

"Tell me, Percy, have you learned any more about the
employee you wrote me about, Wes DuMont?"

"No, sir. Nothing since I wrote you and suggested that
you look into his actions personally in Casper. I hope I
didn't overstep my bounds by making such a request, but
I knew that you would easily be able to do so under the
circumstances—"

"Don't apologize, Percy! It was an excellent suggestion.
I wired our Denver office to see what I could learn about
the man, and this is what I heard back from them." He

reached into his inside jacket pocket, took out a paper, and began reading. "Wes DuMont has been employed by this organization for three years. He has no known family and apparently no close friends. He has received rapid promotion by letters of authorization from the home office in San Francisco and is currently the executive secretary to Mr. Ben Coaltree."

"Then you *did* make him your executive secretary?" Percy asked in surprise.

Coaltree laid the document on the table beside his plate and resumed eating.

"No, I didn't have anything to do with it. I had never heard of the man before you brought him to my attention. But Denver received a letter of complaint from my daughter and sent it along with the information I just read to you. Here, take a look and see what you think." Coaltree took the letter from his jacket and handed it to Percy, who read it quickly, exclaiming with surprise now and again.

"Mr. Coaltree," he said, looking up, "we have long engaged in sharp business dealings, but we have never done anything illegal. It seems that Mr. DuMont has crossed the line of both legality and propriety."

"Yes," Coaltree said. "But on the other hand, I have to give the man credit for ambition and guts. He has started a stage line with virtually no money. I've learned that the Denver office has not been giving him operating funds."

"How has he done it, I wonder. Has he used his own money?"

"I believe he's using the money I sent via our Denver office to be used for my daughter's expenses."

"Then he is a thief as well as a usurper!" Percy said.

"Yes."

"I'll go down to the Western Union office at once, then. I'll send a telegram, discharging him and disbanding the stage line he has established."

"No," Coaltree said firmly, holding up his hand. Then he smiled. "I prefer to do that myself, tomorrow, in person."

"Very well, sir." Percy smiled, too, understanding that his employer had made his own plans. "To turn, then, to a

more pleasant subject. Are you excited over the prospect
of seeing your daughter again?"

"Yes," Coaltree said. "But I also confess to a degree of
anxiety."

"Mr. Coaltree, surely she understands that the long
separation wasn't your fault. It was her mother who took
her away, and her mother who refused to allow you to see
her or even contact her."

"Yes, well, I'm not concerned about that. I'm more
concerned about what has gone on in Casper, in my name,
since she arrived. Her letter clearly shows that she has
allied herself with those against Coaltree."

"Perhaps so, but when you discharge Mr. DuMont tomorrow, that will set things right."

"Will it? I'm going to be asking her to be very forgiving," Coaltree mused. "And to accept a few things that
might be difficult for her to understand."

"I don't know your daughter, of course, but now I've
read two of her letters," Percy replied. "She seems to me
to be a young woman of remarkable sensitivity and sensi-
bility. And don't forget, she *is* your daughter, and there's
something to be said for a family bloodline. Whatever you
ask of her tomorrow, I'm certain she will be understanding."

"I hope so," Coaltree said. "You have no idea how I've
longed for the right to put my arms around her and
welcome her home."

Chapter Twelve

When Big Troy left the Crystal Palace, he cradled his right fist in his left hand. No one else realized it, but he had broken it when he hit the side of the coach. Now it was swelling badly, and the pain was getting worse. When he reached the shop, he tried wrapping it tightly with a bandage and putting it in water, but the swelling and the pain were so severe that he could barely hold a hammer. Still, he had promised Blakely that the stage would be ready, and he intended to see that it was.

Grimacing against the pain and using his left hand as much as possible, Big Troy first removed the broken spokes. Fortunately he had half a wheel in the shop to provide replacements, so the wheel repair went quickly. He was also able to replace the door panel from his salvage stock, and that took even less time. The rest of the damage done by the three thugs was superficial and could be left for another time, but Big Troy still had to build his fire back up to finish the tie rod. He had been saving this task for last, since he knew it would hurt his injured hand more than the other work had.

A short time later, as Big Troy pulled the glowing piece of flat iron from the forge, he heard the sound of a crowd in the street. Knowing it was past suppertime and curious as to why so many people would be in the vicinity of his blacksmith's shop, he stepped outside and saw John Meeker standing in the middle of the street looking toward him.

Meeker had taken off his shirt, and his huge muscles rippled in the summer evening sun.

For a moment, Big Troy recalled the time in Denver six years earlier when John Meeker had stood in the middle of a ring, his sweat-covered body shining as he held his hands over his head in a victory clasp. Tony Rozzelle was prostrate on the canvas, having been pounded senseless by Meeker's powerful fists. The ring, a roped-off square of canvas-covered floor, had been surrounded by more than five thousand spectators, all of whom had come to witness what the papers had billed as "the fight of the ages."

Meeker had been the heavyweight bareknuckle champion of the world, and after he had beaten Tony Rozzelle, a challenge had been issued to all comers. But when the boxing commission had taken a look at the only challenger, Big Troy, and seen his black skin, they had refused him the opportunity to fight for the title.

That had been six years earlier. Now, as Big Troy stood just outside the door of his shop looking at Meeker, he knew the fight was, at last, going to take place.

"Are you ready, Big Troy?" Meeker called.

"Yes, sir, Mista Meeker. I expects the time has come at that." Big Troy took off his apron and then slipped out of his shirt. His muscles were as big as Meeker's and his perspiration gleamed as brightly in the sun. In the excitement no one noticed that Big Troy had winced in pain as he untied his apron. His right hand was so badly swollen that even that simple act was difficult for him.

The fight began without further ceremony. Big Troy and John Meeker circled about, holding their fists doubled in front of them, each trying to test the mettle of the other. Meeker threw the first punch, a clublike swing, which Big Troy leaned away from, counterpunching with a quick left jab. The blacksmith's fist caught Meeker flush on the jaw, but Meeker just laughed it off.

In the next flurry of punches, Meeker hit Big Troy with two powerful lefts, followed by a crushing right hand. Big Troy's ears rang, and he felt his knees weaken. It was the hardest he had ever been hit, and for a moment he was afraid he would go down.

Meeker was astounded that Big Troy was still on his feet. He had connected with as good a blow as he had ever thrown. In over one hundred fights, no opponent had ever stayed on his feet after being hit that hard, and he wondered just what this colored man had in him. He also knew that he had left himself wide open for Big Troy's own right when he threw the punch, and he wondered why Big Troy had not taken advantage of it.

As the fight continued, it became obvious to the crowd that Big Troy was not able to trade blows with Meeker with any degree of parity. Big Troy hit Meeker hard several times with his left hand, and that would have been enough to fell most men, but Meeker was able to back up and shake off the blows. In the meantime, Meeker was punishing Big Troy severely.

By now, many in the crowd had realized why Big Troy was holding back with his right hand. The swollen fingers told them he must have been hurt in the earlier fight. But it was too late now to yell foul play. They could only watch with clinical interest and personal sympathy to see how Big Troy would handle the problem.

Big Troy hit Meeker in the stomach and chest several times, hoping to discover a soft spot, but found none. Giving that up, he returned to throwing left jabs at Meeker's face. The blows were ineffectual until he saw an opening that allowed him to send a quick long left to Meeker's nose. He felt the nose give under his knuckles, and he knew he had broken it. Blood gushed over Meeker's lips and teeth and down his chin, but Meeker just grinned wickedly, seemingly unperturbed by his injury.

Big Troy kept trying to hit the nose again, but Meeker tried just as hard to protect it, and Big Troy was unable to get through. Since Meeker was covering it up, Big Troy knew that at least the nose was hurting. The black man continued to hold back his right, waiting for an opening that would allow him one good blow with the injured hand. He knew he would suffer for it, but he was willing to pay the price.

Meeker apparently had realized along with the yelling crowd that Big Troy was not going to use his right, for he became a little careless. Eager to finish the fight, Meeker started throwing great swinging blows toward Big Troy, just barely missing him. Big Troy knew that if one of them connected soundly, he could be finished.

After four or five such roundhouse attempts, Big Troy noticed that Meeker was leaving a slight opening for a good right hand punch, if he could just slip it in across his shoulder. He timed it just right. On Meeker's next swing, Big Troy threw his straining right fist straight at the place where he thought Meeker's nose would be. He hit the nose perfectly and had the satisfaction of hearing a bellow of pain from Meeker for the first time. It was a bruising punch, but it cost Big Troy; he winced as a sharp pain shot from his right hand through his whole body.

It had been a telling blow, but not a finishing blow, and now Big Troy did not know if he had another punch left in his right hand. He went back to jabbing with his left. He was getting tired. He started moving more slowly, both with his legs and his arms. His right hand was now so badly swollen that he could scarcely hold it up, much less use it.

Meeker must have realized that his advantage had improved, for now he changed tactics, rushing Big Troy, swinging both hands. It was all Big Troy could do to parry the blows. But even that had a telling effect, as his arms and shoulders began to hurt from the punishment he absorbed. Then Meeker landed a short straight right. It was not one of his wild, swinging punches, and Meeker was not positioned perfectly, but the drive and strength of it came directly from his shoulder, and when it crashed against Big Troy's head, the man dropped to the ground like a sack of flour.

Big Troy rolled over and then got to his hands and knees in an attempt to rise. Meeker rushed over and tried to kick him.

"Big Troy, look out!" Crack called in warning, and Big Troy rolled out of the way, just in time. He managed to hop to his feet before Meeker could attempt a second kick, and while Meeker was off balance, Big Troy sent a low, whistling left hook into Meeker's groin.

Meeker dropped both hands to his groin, and Big Troy quickly sent his broken right hand into Meeker's Adam's apple as hard as he could. He jerked his hand back in agony, but it was worth the pain to see Meeker choke and grab his neck with both hands and then fall to his knees. Had Big Troy hit any other man that hard, the man would have choked to death with a crushed esophagus. Meeker survived the blow, though all his strength was taken from him.

With Meeker on his knees, Big Troy attempted to close in and finish him off. To his surprise, however, he discovered that he simply did not have the strength. Instead, he staggered over to a hitching rail, hung onto it for a moment, and then slid to the ground into a sitting position.

The crowd, which had yelled its encouragement to the fighters for the entire battle, now stood in stunned silence. Never had any man or woman present seen such a fight, and they looked at the two spent battlers in absolute awe.

For a long moment, Big Troy and Meeker looked at each other, neither able to rise. Finally Meeker raised his hand, and in a voice made raspy by the blow to his throat, he said, "Mr. Lucas."

"Yes, sir, Mista Meeker?"

"I want you and everyone here to know that I've fought the heavyweight champions of ten countries and three continents, but I never fought a better man than you."

Meeker stretched out his hand, and Big Troy crawled over to grab it. The crowd cheered as the two men embraced.

In the background, Wes DuMont kicked the dirt in anger and stalked away.

*   *   *

The mood of the town, already ebullient over Big Troy's defeat of DuMont's three thugs earlier in the day, was now positively festive. Celebrations that had started in the saloons that afternoon spilled out into the street that night, and old friendships that had been fractured by the competition between the stage lines were mended. Only the brawlers that DuMont had brought in from out of town avoided the celebration, staying together as a sullen little knot of men in one corner, drinking by themselves.

Amy was as happy as everyone else, though her happiness came from a different source. She could scarcely contain the smile on her face, and Marybeth finally had to ask her about it.

"I know you aren't that overjoyed from the outcome of the fight," Marybeth said. "So what turned you into such a bundle of joy?"

"Oh, Marybeth, Smith loves me," Amy said. "I love him and he loves me, and . . . and everything is going to be wonderful! I realize it may sound foolish, but I just know it is!"

Marybeth smiled and hugged Amy. "I'm happy for you, honey. I really am. And I just pray that everything works out the way you want it to."

"Well, of course everything is going to work out," Amy said. "I simply will not allow it to be any other way." Amy looked at Marybeth and then smiled. "And things are going to work out for you, too."

"Work out for me? Why, whatever do you mean?"

"Whatever do I mean?" Amy teased, mocking Marybeth's tone. "You know what I mean. You're in love with Angus, aren't you?" To Amy's surprise, she actually saw a blush of color flame Marybeth's cheeks.

"I suppose I am," Marybeth admitted.

"Good, good. Now, let me tell you what I'm going to do," Amy said. "When my father arrives tomorrow, I'm going to tell him that I want him to close the Coaltree stage line between Casper and Medicine Bow. That way, all of Angus's problems will be over, and you two can get married."

Marybeth laughed. "If only things were that simple," she said. "Your father is a very important, very wealthy man. He may not see this question as you and I do."

"If he ever wants anything to do with me, he'll see it," Amy said.

"Amy, no. Don't commit yourself to such a blind promise. He's your father, and Angus and I are—"

"My friends," Amy interrupted. "My closest, dearest friends in the entire world. Don't forget, Marybeth, I've never even met my father. If my standing up for what I believe is right means never getting to know him, then that's the way it will have to be."

"You are a dear, dear girl," Marybeth said, embracing her again. "I only hope you aren't hurt by all this."

Marybeth was called away from the table by a problem in the kitchen then, and Amy, thinking about what she was going to say to her father, suddenly had an idea. She would go to DuMont and try to make him see that his tactics were not right—and in the process find out how involved her father really was in this business.

It was dark outside, but the street was alive with people who were still celebrating after the big fight. Lanterns had been brought out onto the boardwalk and into the street, and groups of men gathered around them laughing, drinking, and singing. In some cases, they were recreating wobbly versions of the fight.

Amy picked her way along the boardwalk, giving wide berth to the noisiest celebrants, until she came to DuMont's office. Just as she was about to go inside, however, she saw Fast Charlie Payson approaching.

Though suddenly seized by fear, Amy had the presence of mind to duck into the shadows between the Coaltree office and the general store. She knew that DuMont had put up a reward for Payson's capture and conviction, so she was frightened for him as well as for herself. Quietly, she sneaked around to the side window, intending to tap on the pane to get his attention and warn him that Payson was here. Before she could act, however, she saw Payson enter the building and be greeted warmly by DuMont. She was close enough to hear every word.

"It's all over town, what great friends your giant and that nigger are," Payson said.

"Yes," DuMont said. "That was a turn of events I hadn't planned on."

"Doesn't seem that much of anything's been going your way lately, does it?" the albino said. "Maybe I ought to pull out."

"I don't know what you've got to complain about," DuMont replied. "I gave you all the information you needed to rob Hightower's stages, and I didn't ask for a penny of the money."

"Wouldn't have done you any good if you had asked," Payson said. "I wouldn't have given it to you. I took all the risks, so I kept all the money."

"And I even gave you a bonus for killing Billy," DuMont said accusingly.

Outside, Amy could not believe her ears. Marybeth had hinted that perhaps DuMont might be behind the stage holdups, but Billy's killing? My God, was her father employing murderers?

Payson chuckled. "That just means we're even, because I killed Deekus for free. But the point is, you haven't given me a piece of information worth a damn in nearly a week. There hasn't been any money on any of the stages. I figure it's about time for me to move on. That's what I came to tell you."

"No, no," DuMont said. "Don't leave yet. I have one more job for you."

"What is it?"

"It's easy enough," DuMont said. "I want you to meet Hightower's morning stage and kill the driver and shotgun guard. I'll give you one thousand dollars in cash when the job is done."

Payson laughed. "Easy enough way to earn a thousand," he said. "But why do you want them dead?"

"I've run out of time," DuMont said. "The telegrapher

told me Coaltree is coming tomorrow. I think killing those two will be enough to drive the rest of Hightower's men away," DuMont said. "If he has nobody working for him, he has no business. When Coaltree gets here, he'll find his stage line the only one in town."

"All right, DuMont. Give me the thousand dollars, and I'll kill them for you."

"After they're dead."

"Unh-uh," Payson said, shaking his head. "After I kill them, I'm leaving this part of the country. Give me the money now, or I'll just kill you and take it."

"All right, all right," DuMont said, visibly shaken by Payson's warning. "That'll take every cent of available cash I have, but I'll give it to you."

"I thought you might see it my way," Payson hissed, venom in his voice and eyes.

Shocked and terrified by what she had seen and heard, Amy waited until Payson had left the office and ridden off into the night before she returned to the Crystal Palace. Smith saw her when she came in, and he knew from her expression that something had happened. He hurried over and walked her to a table, where she sat down, for the moment too shocked to speak.

"What is it, Amy?" Smith asked. "What's happened?"

Marybeth was at the bar joking with Fred. She looked over at the table and saw Smith and Amy together, and for a moment was going to give the two lovers the time alone. Then she saw the same shock in Amy's face that Smith had seen, and she walked over to discover what was going on.

"It's Wes DuMont," Amy said. "He's been behind everything. He's been giving information to Payson so Payson could hold up Angus's stagecoaches. Oh, and he even paid Payson a bonus when that poor guard, Billy, was killed!"

"I *knew* it!" Marybeth said. "I've known all along Du-Mont was a snake in the grass."

"How did you find all this out?" Smith asked Amy.

"I wanted to talk to DuMont, to ask him if he thought my father would listen to me when I ask him to let Angus operate in peace. I saw Payson going into the building, and I slipped around to the side. I heard everything. . . . I heard them talking about the coaches that had been robbed, the bonus DuMont paid for Billy, and . . . Oh, no!" she gasped, as if suddenly remembering.

"What is it?"

"The morning stage! Smith, Payson is going to meet the morning stage and kill the driver and the guard! DuMont actually believes that if they do that, everyone will quit working for Angus, and DuMont can present my father with an exclusive route between here and Medicine Bow. Oh, how *awful* to think my father would condone such activity."

"Now, now, we don't know that he does," Marybeth said, patting Amy's hand reassuringly. "After all, it was DuMont you overheard, not your father."

"That's true," Smith said. "I think DuMont is the bad apple here. I think this whole thing has been his idea from the beginning."

"I certainly hope so," Amy said. "But listen, we must stop the morning stage. We can't let it leave Casper. We can send a wire to Medicine Bow to tell Angus why we stopped it. Although . . . if we *do* send a wire, DuMont will find out immediately."

"What do you mean?" Marybeth asked.

"DuMont said he knew my father was coming tomorrow because the telegrapher told him."

"I'd be willing to bet that's where DuMont was getting the information about the money shipments, too," Smith said.

"Well, whether he tells or not, we've got to get word to Angus to tell him why the coach won't be running tomorrow."

"But it *is* going to run tomorrow," Smith said.

"What do you mean?"

"It's time this problem was ended for good. I'm taking the stage out," Smith said.

"No!" Marybeth said. "No, you mustn't do that. You can't."

"It has to be done," Smith said.

Amy was shocked by the statement. "What are you saying?" she asked. "Why would you even consider such a thing? Smith, listen to yourself. You're talking like one of these . . . these ruffians. You're a warm, cultured gentleman. You're the man I love! Surely you can see that the best solution is just to keep the morning stage from leaving at all. That way no one gets hurt. With that accomplished, you and I can leave Casper and start a new life together."

"Amy, I can't leave Angus to face a renewed threat in the future. Don't you understand? It's a question of loyalty, love, and honor. 'I could not love thee, dear, so much, lov'd I not honor more,' " he said. It was a quote from an old poem about a young man taking leave of the woman he loved to go off to war.

When she realized what Smith had in mind, Amy burst into tears. She got up from the table and ran to her room, where she threw herself on the bed and cried herself to sleep.

Amy had no idea what time it was when she woke up. A splash of silver spilled in through the window, and when she walked over to look outside, she saw that the town was totally dark. All the celebrants were finally asleep. From her window she could see the livery stable at the far end of the street and, in the shadows, the dark form of the stage. Suddenly she realized what she had to do.

Moving quietly to the door, she looked out into the hall. When she saw no one, she sneaked out, down the stairs. From behind the bar she took a revolver. Then, holding it in the folds of her skirt, she hurried through the cool night air to the livery. There she climbed into the stage, curled up on the floor, and pulled a piece of canvas over herself.

*   *   *

It was still dark when Smith hitched up the team the next morning. He had arranged with the driver and shot-gun guard the night before to take their run. He intended to leave directly from the livery, rather than passing by the Crystal Palace to see if there were any passengers. He wanted to make this run alone. With the horses hitched to the stage, Smith climbed up onto the driver's box and urged the team on. No one who knew him as the piano player would have recognized him on the driver's seat, handling the reins instead of tickling the ivory piano keys. Though he had little experience driving a coach, his natu-ral abilities allowed him to recall the rudiments with ease.

It was more than his position at the reins that made him look different, though. It was also the gun belt around his waist with the pearl-handled, silver-plated Colt .44 in the holster. And instead of wearing a conservative jacket and vest, he had donned a pair of black slacks and a black silk shirt. On his head was a black hat with a small red feather protruding from a silver hatband. He had made the com-plete change from Smith, likable piano player, to Rufus Butler, flamboyant gunfighter.

Because she had not seen Amy since the evening be-fore, when Amy had been crying, Marybeth stopped out-side the young woman's door and knocked lightly. When she heard no response, she called out and knocked harder, at last opening the door to look inside. The room was empty, and when Marybeth realized where Amy might have gone, she gasped.

Ten minutes later, Marybeth was knocking on the door of the small apartment Big Troy had built behind his blacksmith's shop.

"Troy! Big Troy, open up, please!" she called.

The door opened and Big Troy looked out. One of his eyes was swollen completely shut, and there was a ban-dage above his other eye. His lips were also cut and swollen from his fight with Meeker.

"Oh, my heavens," she gasped. She reached up and touched his cheek. "Are you all right?"

"Yes'm," Big Troy said. "But you must be worried 'bout somethin', wakin' me up like this."

"Oh, yes," Marybeth said. "Big Troy, Smith told me you know who he is."

"Yes'm, I knows."

"We learned last night that the albino was planning to kill the driver and guard of the morning stage, so Smith took their place and drove the stage out himself."

Big Troy closed his eyes for a moment in an attempt to calm the throbbing in his head. He had the same faith in Smith going up against Payson as Smith had had in Troy's ability to handle Meeker. He just hoped Smith came out of it looking and feeling better than he did at the moment. "I expects it's somethin' he figured needed doin'."

"Yes, and I know better than to try stopping him. But Amy might be hiding inside that stage, and I'm sure Smith knows nothing about it. I'm afraid she's in great danger, Troy. Please, hitch up a buckboard and take me after them. We've got to catch up to the stage and get her off before Payson meets them."

"All right," Big Troy agreed. "You wait right here, and I'll be right with you."

The sun at his back was well above the horizon when Smith saw two men sitting astride their horses in the middle of the road ahead. He halted the team as he drew near, and then he stepped onto the seat and from there up to the top of the stage. He stood there, his feet slightly spread, looking down at them.

As expected, Payson was one of the riders. The other was Wes DuMont, who for the first time since Smith had known him was wearing a gun.

"What are you doing here, piano player?" DuMont asked derisively, put somewhat off balance by Smith's changed appearance. "Where's the regular driver?"

"Shut up, you idiot," Payson hissed scornfully at Du-Mont. "Don't you know who this is?"

"Of course I know. It's the piano play—"

"It's Rufus Butler," Payson cut him off. All the sensations Payson had felt around the piano player were now explained. He had known there was something about the man. He had sensed something hidden and dangerous, and now he felt some relief to know that his sixth sense had been right on target.

Smith smiled at Payson. "You aren't surprised, are you?" he asked.

"I've prayed for the day we'd meet," Payson replied.

"I'd say that any praying you do today should be for your own future," Smith said, grinning.

Just then a highly polished black coach approached from the direction of Medicine Bow. It was being handled by a liveried driver and appeared to be the private coach of a wealthy magnate or privileged dignitary.

"What's going on here?" the driver of the coach asked as it pulled to a halt.

DuMont pointed to the coach. "Who are you? Who do you have in there?" he asked the driver nervously.

"I am Percy Rawlings. My passenger is Mr. Ben Coaltree. Now, please, move aside."

"We ain't movin' nowhere," Payson snarled at the liveried driver. "We got us some unfinished business to attend to here."

"Fool!" DuMont said to him out of the side of his mouth. "It's all over now, can't you see? That's Mr. Coaltree's private coach."

At that moment the door to Smith's coach opened, and Amy stepped out. Startled, Smith looked down at her. "Amy! Amy, what are you doing here?"

"I . . . I couldn't let you come alone," Amy said. She lifted her hands then, and Smith saw that she was pointing a revolver in the direction of Payson and DuMont.

"Stay out of this," Smith told her. "I've got to do this alone."

"Ready, piano player?" Payson hissed.

Smith looked back at Payson and nodded.

"My God!" DuMont blurted out. "You can't do this! We may as well be in the middle of town. There are too many people."

"It's too late," Payson said, and suddenly he moved for his gun.

He was good, better than anyone Smith had ever faced, maybe even better than Rufus Butler himself. But Smith had one advantage; he was standing, while Payson was on his horse. That enabled Smith to beat Payson by a fraction of a second. Smith fired, catching Payson in the chest. Spinning around, Payson pulled the trigger of his own gun by reflex as he collapsed.

DuMont gasped in pain and surprise as Payson's stray bullet struck him in the belly. The impact tumbled him from his horse, and he joined Payson, who was already dead on the ground.

At that moment the buckboard carrying Big Troy and Marybeth arrived on the scene from the direction of Casper. After the two had climbed down and been filled in on what had happened, Marybeth joined Amy and, cautiously walking behind Big Troy, approached the two men sprawled on the ground.

As Smith climbed down from the stage, Amy ran to him. "Oh, I was so frightened for you," she said.

"You needn't have been frightened for me," Smith said quietly. "Don't you understand now? I'm not who you think I am. I've been playing a role here in Casper."

"Oh?" Amy responded firmly. She looked at him with eyes that were wide with emotion, but full of understanding. "Are you telling me you are not the man who plays the piano so beautifully, night after night? Are you saying you're not the man with a soul sensitive to the troubles of his friends? Are you not the man 'could not love me, so much, lov'd you not honor more'?"

"I am that man," Smith agreed. "But I'm more, Amy. I'm Rufus Butler, also. After the war I became a gun-fighter in circumstances I would rather not recall. I'm not certain I understand my past, even looking back on it now. I tried to put it all behind me here in Casper, but I couldn't stand by any longer without taking some action to stop what was happening. I know, now, that you can't love me, knowing who I am—knowing what I am."

"Oh, Smith—Rufus—whoever you are. I love you! I love *you*, don't you see? You, the man, not your name."

"But you don't understand," Smith said. "Now that my secret is out, more men like Payson will come looking for me."

"That's not necessarily so," a new voice called out, and everyone looked toward the private coach to see Angus Hightower climbing out. But this was a different Angus, so elegantly attired that the people from Casper blinked and looked again.

"Angus!" Marybeth exclaimed. "You're riding with Ben Coaltree. What do you . . ." Her voice trailed off in bewilderment.

Angus cleared his throat. "Well, you see, I *am* Ben Coaltree," he said.

Everyone was speechless for a moment after his revelation.

"I don't understand," Marybeth finally said. "You've been here for over six months. Why were you pretending to be someone you aren't? And why all of this, I mean the competition between the stage lines? If you owned both of them, you could have stopped it."

"No one knew who I was, not even DuMont," he explained. "Especially not DuMont. You see, I had learned of some unusual happenings involving Mr. DuMont, and my disguise allowed me to have an unhindered view of his activities. Also, I've been wanting to build a stage line from scratch again for years; Coaltree Cross-country has grown so large, with so many employees and so much paperwork that, from my perspective, it hardly seemed like a stage line anymore. So I came to Casper and became Angus Hightower. When DuMont showed up, I allowed the competition to begin to see just what he would do." He looked down and said, "I'm afraid I allowed it to get out of hand."

"But why didn't you send someone else to do it? Why did *you* do it all?" Smith wanted to know.

"Why did you pretend to be a man named Smith," Coaltree replied, "when all along you were Rufus Butler, the famous gunfighter?"

"I wasn't proud of Rufus Butler," Smith said.

"Well there you have it. I wasn't proud of Ben Coaltree, either. Besides, as Ben Coaltree, all the fun had gone out of life. Building an empire was rewarding, but owning one was not. So, with the help of a few trusted friends—most notably Percy, here—I have, from time to time, assumed other identities." He looked at Marybeth. "I never found an identity that so suited me as the one of Angus Hightower, though. And I've never found a woman I loved as much as I love you. You have to believe that."

Marybeth smiled. "Angus, you can change who you say you are . . . but I don't believe there's any way you can change what you are. I know what you are, and that is the man I've fallen in love with."

"Amy?" Coaltree said. "Amy, darlin', can you accept me? What do you think?"

Amy, still dazed from the roar of the gunplay and the back-to-back revelations of Smith and Angus, ran her hand through her hair and looked at the man who had just told her that he was her father.

"I . . . I don't know. Why didn't you tell me?"

"I surely intended to," Coaltree said. "And again, honey, I'm sorry. But when DuMont started running roughshod over Wyoming Rapid Express, and doing it in my name, I decided to stay in disguise a while longer, just to see how far he would actually go. I had no idea he would involve Payson in his schemes. I'm afraid I almost waited too long. And if I've damaged what you and I had between us as Angus and Amy, then I did wait too long."

Amy looked at him for a long moment; then she smiled and threw her arms around his neck. "You know, the funny thing is that I often found myself wishing you were my father," she said. "Now that it's true, I'm too happy to be upset about anything else."

"Angus . . . uh, Mr. Coaltree," Smith began.

Coaltree held up his hand. "I'd still like to be called Angus," he said. "If I don't have to, I don't intend to ever go back to being Ben Coaltree. And unless I miss my guess, you would just as soon not be known as Rufus Butler."

"That's right," Smith said. "You said I wouldn't necessarily have to spend the rest of my life looking over my shoulder. Do you have an idea?"

"Yes." Coaltree pointed to DuMont's body. "I've done a little research on our friend, Wes DuMont. He's an orphan, with no known relatives and few friends, if any. I could find a suitable explanation for his continued absence from the office in Denver. Now, then, if he were found wearing a hat with a silver band and red feather, and if he had a pearl-handled, silver-plated gun, reasonable people might conclude that all this time Rufus Butler has been hiding out in our very town, passing himself off as Wes DuMont. You could drive the coach back to Casper with the bodies on board, and everyone here will confirm that DuMont-Butler fought it out with Payson, and the two men shot each other. We could bury Rufus Butler forever, and we here would be the only ones who would know."

Smith looked over at the driver of Coaltree's coach, with a question in his eyes.

"Percy Rawlings is my most trusted confidant," Coaltree assured him. "I trust him with both my money and my life."

That summer, newspaper reporters from all over the state covered the funerals of two of the most feared gunfighters in the West. The bodies were transported down the main street of Casper in two highly polished hearses. People lined both sides of the street, and fathers lifted little children to their shoulders. Sixty years later, those children would tell their grandchildren that they had witnessed the funerals of Fast Charlie Payson and Rufus Butler.

Soon after the funerals, Smith accepted a position as Ben Coaltree's personal assistant. Eventually his job would be to oversee the operation of Coaltree Cross-country Express. This would allow Percy Rawlings to retire, and Ben Coaltree to continue living quietly as Angus Hightower. It was a very responsible job, but Coaltree knew that his future son-in-law was a very responsible man.

Smith's first assignment was to announce the closing of Coaltree's line between Casper and Medicine Bow. The taciturn Coaltree offered no explanation of this abrupt action, but Angus Hightower immediately capitalized on it by hiring the Coaltree employees and buying up his carriages and stock.

Angus Hightower and Marybeth Staley had a summer wedding, attended by the employees of Wyoming Rapid Express and by friends from Casper and Medicine Bow. Among the cards and letters from well-wishers was one especially prized, signed by the legendary recluse Ben Coaltree.

FIFTH ANNIVERSARY
SPECIAL EDITION

STAGECOACH

STATION 37:

SHAWNEE
by Hank Mitchum

When thirty-five-year-old Tim Ryan hires a house-keeper to travel from Virginia to his Wyoming ranch, he envisions a matronly woman of advanced age who will give his motherless daughters the proper feminine upbringing. Instead he gets Elizabeth Bradley, a spirited twenty-six-year-old blond widow with a nine-year-old son. Nothing about Elizabeth is matronly. While both she and Ryan are uncomfortable with their situation, they endure it, although the increasing friction between them causes problems, especially when Elizabeth is courted by Ryan's nemesis, George Bigelow.

Friction grows on a grander scale in the community of Shawnee when two homesteaders lose their barn to fire—clearly a case of arson with the cattlemen the prime suspects. Though a cattleman himself, Ryan believes the land should be open to all, a view that makes him unpopular with a good number of his colleagues, chief among them George Bigelow. He also disagrees with Bigelow about the nearby Indians, whom Ryan has befriended.

Despite the growing conflict between the cattlemen and the homesteaders, the strongest tension is created by the combination of desire and stubborn dislike that Elizabeth and Ryan feel for each other— and the culmination of both conflicts cause major upheaval in the town of Shawnee.

Read SHAWNEE, on sale September 1988 wherever Bantam books are sold.